39 Castles: BOOK THREE

THE WHITE CASTLE

Matt Thorne

faber and faber

First published in 2005
by Faber and Faber Limited
3 Queen Square London WC1N 3AU

Typeset by Faber and Faber
Printed in England by Mackays of Chatham plc,
Chatham, Kent

A CIP record for this book
is available from the British Library

ISBN 0-571-22000-2

2 4 6 8 10 9 7 5 3 1

For Charlotte Sinclair

DOWN WITH THE CASTLE FIVE

Arguments against the Castle Five:

What are they doing for us?

⋄ They take our resources,
  disrespect the barter system,
  and live in luxury.

⋄ They have fostered links with
  a series of dangerous individuals
  and caused our Community to be
  invaded for the first time in living
  memory.

Castle Five: The Members

Jonathan: Eleanor's father. Long, sandy hair. Dresses in old work-clothes, and is a kind man, but still getting used to his new position.

Alexandra: the female leader. She is in her mid-twenties with fine, honey-coloured hair and blue eyes. She is trustworthy and considerate.

Sarah: the great-great-granddaughter of the last princess before the fall of the kingdom. She is serene, reserved and full of secrets.

Lucinda: she used to work in an Inn. Kind to Eleanor and always sympathetic, but a young-seeming adult.

Zoran: the joker of the group. Always looking for a good night out and not to be trusted with even the simplest tasks.

CASTLE FACTFILES

Plan

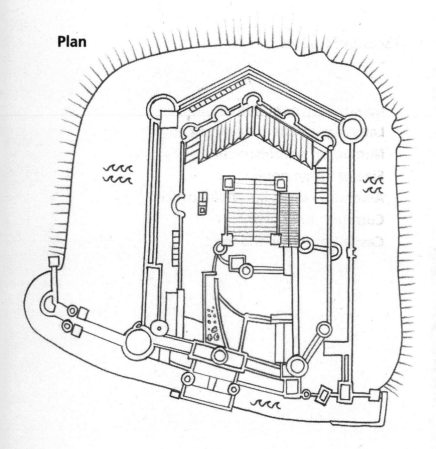

THE WHITE CASTLE

Facts and Figures

Community population: none
Language spoken: none/unknown
Number of schools: none
Size of army: none
Access to castle: limited/unofficial
Currency: unknown
Castle library: abandoned

THE WHITE CASTLE

This book takes place in a future that seems like the past. After the fall of the kingdom, everyone in England has divided themselves into thirty-nine communities, each arranged around a different castle, apart from those who have chosen to live in the wilderness . . .

Chapter One

'So what happened next?'

Eleanor and Mary exchanged a look. 'Next?'

'Yes,' shouted another child. 'Eleanor went to the Greengrove Castle and got put in prison by Basker, then you were kidnapped by Anderson and taken to the Kingmaker's Castle, but what happened after that? What was your next adventure?'

'Oh,' said Eleanor, 'it hasn't happened yet.'

Eleanor and Mary both felt downhearted as they made their way home from the place by the river where the more rebellious children hid from their parents during afternoons after school. For the last two weeks they had been the centre of attention, entertaining everyone with stories about their travels, but as had become obvious today the group had grown bored of their storytelling and it was clear that tomorrow morning everyone would go back to listening to music and staring at the sky. This made them sad because in the retelling of their adventures they had experienced an excitement almost as great as leaving their community for real, and without this it became even more frustrating that the Castle Five – as they now numbered, having lost one member on each of their previous outings – seemed to be in no hurry to set off on another mission.

As they walked past a small clump of trees, Eleanor asked Mary, 'What's that? Pinned to the trunk.'

Mary turned quickly, her red hair getting caught in her mouth. 'It's a poster.'

'Yes,' said Eleanor patiently, 'but what does it say?'

Mary walked over and pulled it from the trunk. She handed it to Eleanor:

Down With The Castle Five
· · · · ·

For some time, we have been asked to have respect for this elitist group without ever being told what exactly it is that they are doing for us.

They take our resources, disrespect the barter system, and live in luxury in a castle that could provide accommodation for far more deserving members of the Community.

In return, they have fostered links with a series of dangerous individuals and caused our Community to be invaded for the first time in living memory.

Anderson, who created the group in the first place, now resides in the Clearheart Castle dungeon and it is clear that the group has outlived its usefulness.

Anyone who agrees that something has to be done is invited to join a public meeting at nightfall tomorrow at Clearheart School.

Do not be intimidated, friends, change is coming.

·

Eleanor read this aloud to Mary, then scrunched it up and threw it on the ground. Mary asked, 'What are we going to do?'

'Don't panic. I'll talk to my father.'

As they walked back to Eleanor's house, they noticed that there were posters everywhere, pasted to walls and pinned to every tree. They pulled down as many as they could, and threw them away. Eleanor kept one to show her father, just in case he didn't believe her. When they came to Mary's house, Eleanor said goodbye to her friend and told her not to worry.

Eleanor couldn't take her own advice. Her father was a gentle man most of the time, but she did feel scared about how he might respond to this sort of attack. She also knew it was important that her mother didn't see the poster. Her parents had not been getting on well since they had returned from the Kingmaker's Castle, and she knew that April, her mother, would seize upon something like this and tell them both to give up on the Castle Five. Eleanor understood how she felt; it couldn't have been fun to have been stuck home on her own while both her husband and daughter were off having adventures, but it didn't help that she was so angry with them now they were back with her. She talked about their visits to other communities as if it was something in their past, something that was over, that would never happen again. 'Now that you're back here, now that you're not gallivanting all over the country on pointless missions, things will get back to normal,' she would say, 'and both of you need to pull your weight.' While she was sympathetic to her mother, Eleanor knew her father felt as frustrated as she did that there were no upcoming missions, and she worried about how to explain what she had seen.

'Dad,' she said as she entered the house, 'I was out with Mary and . . .'

He interrupted her. 'I know,' he said. 'I've seen it. There's a meeting tonight.'

'Really?' she asked, her heart lifting.

'Yes. We'll pick up Mary on the way.'

Eleanor put on her silver dress to go to the meeting. Her mother didn't like her wearing the clothes the Castle tailor had made for her when she was at home, and had run up several new outfits for her to wear instead. These clothes were drab and functional, but Eleanor didn't complain, wanting her mother to be happy. Tonight, though, the memories immediately returned and she felt she wouldn't know how to cope if they didn't go somewhere soon. It was less than a month since their return to the Community, but already her itchy feet were almost unbearable.

Mary was surprised, and pleased to see them. Her

parents invited them inside and asked Jonathan what had brought him there. He explained, and Mary's mother said, 'We don't think like that, you know. Even if Mary hadn't joined the group, we'd always be grateful to you for getting her back from that horrible man.'

'Thank you, Diana,' he said. 'It's only a small minority who have got together to attack us. I'm sure it will all be sorted out soon.'

Her father came forward. 'Will Mary be back late tonight?'

'No,' said Jonathan, 'we shouldn't be gone more than a couple of hours. And I give you my personal guarantee that she will come home safely.'

Simply being inside the Castle again was exciting to Eleanor. Although she was allowed to visit it whenever she wanted, this was the first time she had returned since their last adventure.

'It's fantastic, isn't it?' she remarked to Mary.

'What?'

'Being here again.'

Mary was amused by Eleanor's excitement, pleased that she didn't know that she had visited the Castle several times in the last weeks, for reasons that her friend would not discover for some time. She was glad to be meeting the group properly again, and hoped that this might be the start of another mission. The last time she had left her community it had been as Anderson's hostage, and this time she was keen to go as a willing explorer.

The two girls noticed Hephzibah and her boyfriend Michael waiting by the spiral staircase just inside the entrance. Eleanor breathed in as she saw Hephzibah, who seemed to have changed dramatically in appearance since the last time she'd seen her. Her brown hair was longer than it'd been before, very loosely tied with a small piece of red material. She wasn't wearing clothes designed by the Castle tailor, but instead an expensive-looking pink-and-blue checked blouse. Eleanor wondered who had made it for her. Michael also looked older, proudly sporting the black tunic with a brass bear that Robert had given him before departing to rule the Kingmaker's Castle. Eleanor hadn't seen her friends since she'd got back, and rushed over to embrace Hephzibah. As she did so, another surprise: a sudden blast of perfume.

'Where's Beth?' asked Eleanor.

'She's quit,' said Michael, shrugging.

'What?'

'She said she doesn't want to travel with us any more,' explained Hephzibah. 'She thinks the Castle Five are idiots, I'm a bitch, and Michael is my doting puppy.'

Mary giggled. Eleanor looked at her, then back at

Hephzibah and Michael. 'What do your parents think?'

'My parents are delighted. As far as they're concerned, they've got one daughter back and are now waiting for me to come to my senses.'

'But I don't understand,' said Eleanor. 'Your parents love coming to the Castle.'

'Not any more,' Hephzibah replied, 'they have new friends now. And the hippest thing anyone can do right now is slag us off.'

Eleanor's father seemed agitated by this conversation, and said to the four of them. 'We should go up.'

They climbed the spiral staircase to the third level, going through to the large, candlelit room where Eleanor had been taken on her very first visit to the Castle. The others had already assembled. The remaining child, Stefan, was sitting on one side of the banqueting table. Facing him were the other four members of the Castle Five. Zoran, who was leaning back in his chair with his boots on the table, had a heavier beard than usual, the trademark stubble having grown into a short grey-and-white goatee, with lighter whiskers on the remaining portion of his face. He was wearing his usual dark glasses, even though he was inside and it was night. He looked sad and Eleanor could tell he missed Robert, his old partner-in-crime, who had departed to oversee the Kinder Castle. Alongside Zoran sat Alexandra, who had traded the black dresses she recently favoured for a grey pinafore. Her fine, honey-coloured hair was shorter than before and held back with a white Alice band. Her face looked serious, and Eleanor looked to Sarah, who in many ways most accurately reflected the emotional temperament of the group. She looked less depressed than Zoran or Alexandra, but her face betrayed a determination that made Eleanor anxious. It was clear this meeting wasn't going to be fun. Even Lucinda, the group's light sprite, lacked her usual gaiety, her face now marked with the nasty scar she gained at the battle of Baldwin Castle, although she smiled at Eleanor as she sat down.

'OK,' said Alexandra, 'it's clear that we have a serious problem here that needs to be resolved. We will have another meeting the day after tomorrow to discuss our next move, but for the moment, we have only one aim. Someone needs to infiltrate tomorrow's meeting at the Clearheart School and find out how serious this threat is.'

Hephzibah put her hand up. 'Beth's going.'

Eleanor expected the group to be shocked by this, but they accepted the information without surprise.

'I could go with her,' Hephzibah suggested. 'I could pretend that I hate the Castle Five too.' She seemed to notice the group wince at her words and added, 'Only pretend.'

'No,' said Alexandra, 'she won't believe you.'

'What about me?' said Eleanor. 'I was the one she

came to when she had a crush on Michael. The two of us haven't got on as well as we used to recently, but . . .'

Alexandra shook her head. 'That won't work either. Don't take this the wrong way, Eleanor, but no one would believe that you'd turned against us. You're too loyal. But,' she said, 'Mary, she hardly knows you, and she seems to be as big a fan of Katharine as you were of Anderson.'

Eleanor shuddered at the mention of Katharine, Anderson's girlfriend, and a woman she had never trusted, ever since she caused her to be imprisoned at the Greengrove Castle. She looked at Mary, who seemed pleased to have been singled out for duty.

'Good. You don't have much time. And it can't be obvious. Are you in her class at school?'

'No,' said Mary, 'we don't even go to the same school. She goes to Beacon Rise, not Clearheart's.'

'Ah,' said Alexandra, 'then this could be difficult.'

'Not necessarily,' Hephzibah argued. 'I could go home and talk about how I didn't trust Mary, how she'd seemed a bit evasive recently, that I was worried she might even go to the meeting. I could say it all as if I was totally disgusted, and then if Mary bumped into her, accidentally on purpose, on the way to the meeting, Beth might be a bit suspicious at first, but I reckon she'd buy it. She's so keen to have an ally I think she'd be too excited to think about it too much.'

'What do you think, Mary?' asked Alexandra. 'Could you convince her you hate us?'

Mary nodded. 'I'll just tell her some of the things Anderson said to me when he kidnapped me.'

This was the end of the meeting. Eleanor and Mary walked back to her house with Eleanor's father. Then, after she had been safely returned to her parents, Jonathan and Eleanor walked back home in the moonlight.

'What do you think of the plan?' Jonathan asked Eleanor.

'It should go OK,' she replied. 'I think Beth will believe Mary.'

He nodded. 'And you trust Mary?'

'Of course. Completely. She's my friend.'

'Yes,' said Jonathan, 'all that bad stuff is in the past now.'

'What bad stuff? Anderson and Katharine? Her head got turned for a minute, that's all. It wasn't her fault.'

He rubbed his daughter's hair. 'You're right, Eleanor. I'm sorry; I don't know why I had any doubts. Everything will work out fine.'

CHAPTER
TWO

Mary hung from the tree, watching Beth walk up the muddy path towards her. She swung down from one of the highest branches and dropped onto the ground. Beth came closer, struggling to see her in the dusk.

'What are you doing?' she asked.

Mary rubbed her hands together. 'Nothing. Killing time.'

Beth gave her a long stare. Mary could tell she was suspicious, but felt determined to play it cool. Beth said, 'I thought you went down by the river after school?'

'I do. I was there earlier. Now I'm here.'

'Yes. But why are you here?'

'I didn't want to go alone. I was waiting here in case anyone I knew came by.'

'Go where alone?'

Mary considered her tactics. She knew what she had been told to do, but thought she should handle it her own way, however risky. 'Hephzi said . . .'

Beth scowled. 'So my sister's a blabbermouth as well as a bitch. She was saying all sorts of stuff about you too.'

'I know. She's never liked me. She told Ellie to stop being friends with me.' Mary stopped, worried she'd gone too far. It was hard to lie about another person's sibling. Especially twins, who were supposed to know each other's every thought and have a special psychic connection. But she seemed to have got away with it.

'She wants to get between you,' said Beth, having accepted this story. 'Didn't you realise she's jealous of your friendship? She hates the way the two of us are always left on our own together all the time just because we're twins. Hephzi's almost as big a goody-goody as Eleanor. The two of them deserve each other.'

'I thought you and Ellie were friends.'

Beth frowned. 'We used to be. Until she betrayed me.'

'How did she betray you?'

'Come on,' said Beth, 'it's getting late. Let's walk to the meeting and I'll explain along the way.'

Mary smiled, delighted at the way Beth had accepted she was going to the meeting and stopped challenging her. She liked Beth, and felt relieved that she could fulfil her role without having to fake her emotions too much. In open defiance of the Castle Five's elegance, she was wearing a dirty red T-shirt, black work trousers and heavy leather boots. Her brown hair was pulled back in a tight bun.

As they walked towards Clearheart School, Beth asked, 'What do you think about Michael?'

'Hephzi's boyfriend? He's fit.'

'Exactly. But he's also weak-willed. Before he met my sister he was podgy and nervous. There was an attraction between us, but I didn't think he was quite good-looking enough to be my boyfriend. Then he started training and, pow, everything changed. But before I'd had chance to tell him how I felt about him, my sis had swooped in and stolen him.'

'That's terrible.'

'I know. And it gets worse. When I went on our second mission, to the Kingmaker's Castle, I told Eleanor about this and asked her to help me. All I wanted her to do was talk to Michael and just hint to him that everything would be OK and no one would judge him if he ditched Hephzibah and started going out with me.'

'What did she do?'

'First Eleanor told me he was definitely in love with my sister, even though he'd told her he also had feelings for me. Then when I'd had enough of all of them and went off for a talk with Katharine she got Michael to come find me and . . . well, she really embarrassed me in front of him. Which way do we go now?'

'Oh yeah, I forgot, you don't go to this school. It's not far now. Down this lane . . .' Mary led the way and Beth followed her. 'Do you know where the meeting is being held?'

'On the playing field, I think.'

The pair of them noticed a row of flaming torches, marking out a pathway. In the distance there was a small gathering, mainly figures dressed in brown hooded cloaks.

'So, do you like this school?' Beth asked.

'Well, I've got nothing to compare it to. I used to like it, when Eleanor and I went together, before she got involved with the Castle, but after that everything started to seem meaningless. None of our teachers tell us the truth about everything, and it's not because they're deliberately keeping it from us, it's because they don't know themselves. Hardly any of the teachers from our school have been outside the Community, they don't know what's out there.'

'Do you think that's such a bad thing?'

'Yes. I know you don't like the Castle Five, Beth, and I don't either, that's why I'm here, but I am interested in finding out the truth about stuff. About our country's history, and the other communities . . .' She looked at Beth, worried she was losing her.

'Yes,' said Beth, 'I agree. The reason why I'm against the Castle Five isn't because they travel, but because they don't do anything with their knowledge. They should be strengthening our community, but they haven't made any attempt to share their experience with the normal people who live here.'

Their conversation came to a natural pause, and rather than attempting to reignite it Mary and Beth looked at each other again, and Mary realised that a genuine bond had been formed. There were others walking alongside them now, and she felt intimidated by the serious atmosphere. Until now she had seen her mission as little more than a game, but now she felt afraid that someone might challenge her.

A man in a hooded cloak stood at the entrance to the playing field. He held an ink pen and a piece of parchment. When Mary and Beth passed next to him, he said, 'Can I have your names please?'

'Mary Reece.'

'Beth Coles.'

'Thank you.'

He stood back and let them walk on. Mary wondered if there would be anyone she knew from the Community at this meeting. It was getting darker now and as they joined the crowd the sense of excitement was infectious. She whispered to Beth, 'There's lots of people here, isn't there?'

'That's because everyone agrees with us. The Castle Five are so arrogant. This is going to come as such a shock to them.'

A thought occurred to Mary. 'Beth, did you have anything to do with organising this meeting?'

The other girl shook her head. 'No. They asked me to

speak, to give a first-hand account of how little the Castle Five have managed to achieve, but I said I wanted to wait until the movement had gathered strength. We have to get the possibility of rebellion into everyone's heads first. Then we can build on that sense of discontent with hard facts.'

Mary nodded, wanting to show agreement even though she didn't completely understand Beth's argument.

The group was assembling in front of a small, illuminated, makeshift stage. People were jostling for position, and there was a loud murmuring as everyone chatted in an excited manner. Mary realised that for many of these people this was an important social occasion.

'Besides,' Beth added, 'the person who started all this is nearly as close to the Castle Five as I am.'

As she said this, another brown-robed figure came out onto the stage. The crowd fell silent and the figure cast back her hood. Mary gasped in surprise, and Beth looked at her and winked. The person on stage was Eleanor's mother, April.

'Hello,' she said in a loud voice, 'thank you for coming. There are still lots of people arriving so if you could pack yourselves together as closely as possible . . .' She laughed as the crowd moved forward. 'Maybe not that tight.'

April was standing in the centre of a spotlight beam. 'We are gathered here tonight because for too long now we as a community have been denied a voice. Now I don't presume to speak on your behalf, and the only reason I am up here tonight is to tell you about my experiences with the Castle Seven . . . Six . . . Five . . . however many of them there are this week.' This got a laugh. 'I first met Anderson . . .'

Someone in the crowd hissed at the mention of his name.

'I know exactly how you feel,' she said. 'Anyway, I first met him when he came to my house to ask my daughter to join his group. He didn't seek my permission, or my husband's, but simply informed us that she had been chosen and that she would be taken out of school to participate in their peculiar training programme. It was made very clear to me that I had no say in the matter, and that this was a great honour. Later, Anderson directly endangered my daughter's life, thanks to the arrangements he had made with Basker, a man you all know has been creating tremendous problems for our country owing to his incredible lust for power. When the Castle Seven returned from their first mission, after they had been betrayed by Anderson and Katharine, instead of abandoning their foolish group, as might be reasonably expected, they approached my husband Jonathan and asked him to join them. The reason why they did this was because he was the one who, along with my daughter, Eleanor, got them out of the mess they had created for themselves at the Greengrove Castle. Of course he was flattered by their advances, and agreed to join. Now, I understand that some of you might think that I am against the Castle Five for purely personal reasons, that I'm some lonely woman who dislikes my family going off without me, but that is not the case. What angers me, and I have gained this insight from watching my husband and daughter, and listening to their stories after they returned from their visit to the insufferable so-called intellectuals at the Kingmaker's Castle is that they are abusing their position and presenting an image of the Clearheart Community to surrounding communities that none of us would be happy with.

'We are humble people, who work hard and love our families more than ourselves. We are a community of mothers and fathers, sons and daughters. Yes, we would be interested to meet people in other communities that share our values, but we have no desire to be represented by fools. My husband is a good man, but his head has been turned. And what about the other members of the Castle Five? Zoran is a notorious drunk, no stranger to the inns of our land and regularly to be found face-down in the forest, sleeping off another evening of overindulgence. Lucinda is a former barmaid and a woman of dubious moral standing. Alexandra is more interested in the outfits the Castle tailor makes for her than in good, honest toil. Sarah, as I'm sure some of you will already know, is the great-great-granddaughter of the last princess before the fall of the kingdom and, as such, is interested in resurrecting the network of privilege and corruption that used to blight our fair nation.'

Mary was astonished to hear April talking like this. Lots of her phrases didn't sound quite right, as if she was choosing them to please her audience. Mary suddenly thought of her own parents and wondered if they were among this crowd. Her mother and father weren't that close to April, but they had seen her a couple of times when Mary had been taken away from the Community by Anderson. She felt disappointed in April – in spite of her protests, it was obvious she was doing this because she was jealous of her daughter and her husband – but at the same time she admired her ability to come here and address a crowd with such confidence.

Although Mary had been pleased that Eleanor had arranged for her to join the children who travelled with the Castle Five, the excitement of being part of this group was nowhere near as intense as the way she'd felt when Anderson had given her his undivided attention. The things he said to her, like how one day she would rule England, and the way he'd boosted her confidence made her feel that she was letting him down, even though she knew he didn't think that. But it was hard to live up to someone's faith in you, and she couldn't help thinking that just muddling along as Eleanor's best mate was beneath her.

'I wrote on my posters that something has to be done. This is harder than it seems. We have no authorities to appeal to, aside from the army, who will be reluctant to fight the Castle Five. But I believe that if we continue to have meetings, and spread the word, we can appoint our own leaders, and they can challenge the Castle Five. It may even be necessary to foster connections with another community . . . I'm not sure which one yet . . . in order to convince the Castle Five that we are not happy with the way they have represented our community. I am open to all suggestions . . . one possible option is that we have a lottery to decide who gets to visit other castles. Alternatetively, we could have an election and people would get to choose who represents them. We could even say to Alexandra and the others that they could also stand for this position and allow the public to decide if they think they are doing a good job. If these suggestions sound vague, it is because I am not going to speak for you, as that would make me just as conceited as they are. Instead, this is the beginning of a process of discussion and debate that could continue for several months. At the end of that time, we will have a meeting and come to some conclusions. Until then, feel free to express your opinions, and tell your friends and neighbours about these events, which will be advertised in the same manner. Tonight, there is food and drink for everyone, courtesy of Gordon and Hilary Smythe, and later we will have music. Enjoy yourselves, friends, introduce yourselves to your neighbours and let's see some of the community spirit the Castle has tried, and so far failed, to extinguish.'

There was loud applause, continuing for several minutes. Mary had been disappointed by the end of April's speech, as it seemed too woolly compared to the strong way she had started, but on looking around she realised that April had judged the crowd's mood exactly. Rebellion was scary, especially to those used to order. She forgot that, unlike her, most of these people had never been outside their own community, and were only agitated by the sense that they were missing out. April had given them a promise of excitement in their future, but also allowed them time to get used to the idea. And in the meantime, they had food and drink.

Beth took her arm. 'Let's get something to eat.'

'OK.'

They followed the crowd to where Gordon and Hilary Smythe had set up their barbecue. As they were waiting, a woman handed them both drinks. Mary spotted April making her way towards them. She felt scared, but Mary was smiling warmly. When she came close enough, she grabbed Mary's arm.

'Mary, thank you for coming. I had no idea that you would be interested in our group.'

In the light from the flaming torches, Mary could see that April's face was covered with a thin sheen of perspiration. Her eyes were bright.

'I came with Beth.'

'That's great. Would you like to do a talk with her at some later date? You could both give your experiences of being with the Castle Five and explain how and why you fell out with them.'

'Um,' said Mary, 'the thing is, I'm still with them.'

April frowned for a moment, then gave her an even brighter smile. 'A double agent! Excellent.' She tapped the side of her nose. 'I understand. You don't want to give the game away. Well, don't worry, your secret's safe with me.'

Another woman started talking to April and she turned away, leaving Mary and Beth alone. They reached the front of the queue and were handed plates of barbecued chicken and beans. Taking their food, the two girls walked away from the crowd and found a place to sit down.

'I've enjoyed tonight,' Beth told Mary.

'Me too,' she replied. 'Thanks for going to the meeting with me.'

Beth smiled, and touched her arm. They ate their

food and Mary felt happy, forgetting about her complicated mission and enjoying the simple thrill of finding a
new friend.

Eleanor and Jonathan sat in the kitchen, waiting for April to come home. Although they didn't yet know that April had instigated the uprising against the Castle Five, they had both quickly guessed that she had gone to the meeting.

'I can't believe she hasn't even attempted to hide it,' Jonathan had said to Eleanor when they came home to find her gone. They'd spent the afternoon training, just the two of them, mainly to combat the notion that the future of the Castle Five might be in doubt. Her mother had clearly been excited, and left the house in a hurry, as her clothes were strewn over the bed and across chairs.

'What's going to happen, Dad?' Eleanor asked.

'Nothing,' he replied. 'We'll wait until she comes home and then ask her to explain herself.'

So that's what they had been doing, for nearly six hours now. It was getting really late and Eleanor wanted to go to bed, but at the same time she needed to hear her mother's explanation. She knew it was a forlorn hope, but she prayed her mother hadn't been at this meeting, that she'd been out with friends instead. The idea that she could be so disloyal distressed Eleanor. They were supposed to be a family.

Eleanor's eyes were closing when she heard the door open. Suddenly awake, she felt a shudder of fear as her father jumped out of his seat and grabbed April by the shoulder.

'Ow,' she said, trying to shake free, 'get off!'

'You're drunk!' he shouted.

'No, I'm not. I had a few cups of punch, but that's all. How come you're both still up?'

'We were waiting for you.'

'Oh,' she said. 'Why?'

'Because we know where you've been, and we want an explanation.'

'Well, if you know where I've been you don't need an explanation.'

'Mum,' Eleanor cried, 'how could you?'

'Oh, Eleanor, don't be stupid. You must've known this couldn't go on for ever. And, besides, what makes you so special?'

'Don't talk to her like that,' said Jonathan.

'You!' shouted April. 'You're telling me how to talk to my daughter? Why don't you tell her about Alexandra?'

'What about her?'

'Tell her the truth, Jonathan. Tell her the only reason you joined that silly group of hers is so you could have an affair.'

'That's ridiculous, April.'

'Is it?'

'Yes. Is that what all this is about? You've turned the whole Community against us because you're jealous of a non-existent relationship? Oh, April, what have you done?'

Usually Eleanor was frightened when her parents fought, and often hid in her bedroom to avoid hearing their angry voices. But tonight, because she was part of this fight, she didn't cower, but instead faced her father and said in a serious voice, 'Dad, I'm going to ask you something and I need you to tell me the truth. Is Mum right? Are you having an affair with Alexandra?'

In the moment before he responded Eleanor realised she had no idea how he would answer. She had a sudden flashback to the time at the Kingmaker's Castle when she and Hephzi's boyfriend Michael had been going for a midnight walk and had run into Alexandra and Jonathan walking together. She'd had a conversation with Alexandra as they'd walked back to their bed-rooms, and she'd said something, what was it? *He makes me laugh. But only when we're alone together.* Had that meant something more than she thought at the time?

'No,' he said, 'I can put my hand on my heart and tell

you, Eleanor . . . tell both of you . . . that I am not having an affair with Alexandra. She is a good friend, but that's all. I'm ashamed of you, April, being so petty about me having a friendship with another woman. And turning against your family in this way.'

April ignored him. 'Eleanor, it's very late. I understand that you were waiting up for me, but I'm home now and it's time for you to go to bed.'

Eleanor did as she was told, worried that if she didn't she would say something to her mother that she would later regret.

Eleanor lay awake listening to her parents argue for another hour, and then even when they had come to a temporary pause and gone to bed, she couldn't sleep. She changed into her nightdress and extinguished her candle, but it didn't make any difference. Any previous tiredness had gone. She was wishing so hard for something to relieve the boredom of her insomnia that when there was a sudden tap on the window she thought she'd imagined it. But then it came again, two hard taps on the glass. What if it was Anderson? He was the only person who'd tapped on her window before. Had he escaped from the dungeon? Frightened, she sat up and looked through the glass. She could see a face, but not clearly enough to know who it was. She opened the window, and heard a voice say, 'Eleanor, is this your room?'

'Justin!' she called out, astonished. 'Wait there. I'll put on some clothes and come out.'

Eleanor's heart beat fast as she ran to her drawers and quickly pulled out something to wear. It was her white dress, the one she'd worn on the first day they'd met, when she'd emerged from her bedroom at the Greengrove Castle, stepped out onto the circular walkway and spotted one of the first boys she'd ever found attractive. Justin was also the first boy she'd ever kissed, and while she hadn't seen him in months she still thought of him as her boyfriend and was eager to find out if he felt the same way.

She crept through the house, desperately worried that she might wake her parents. She eased the front door open and walked out into the night, looking for Justin. He was standing by his horse, with his back to Eleanor. As she closed the front door he turned round and smiled at her. Eleanor rushed towards him, almost knocking him over as she embraced him with all her strength. Her lips sought his and he kissed her back passionately. She was surprised to feel faint wisps of facial hair tickling her nose, and she wondered if he had been travelling.

They both stepped back. His lightly curled brown hair was longer than when she last saw him, now brushing his shoulders, and his face seemed different too. His features were still fine – soft, delicate lips, a thin nose, and blue eyes – but there was something new there: something of the hard determination of his father, Basker.

It should have frightened Eleanor, but instead she felt intrigued and wanted to know what had happened to him in the time they had been apart.

He gestured to his horse and she climbed on behind him, wrapping her arms around his waist.

'Where are we going?' she asked.

'Not far. I just don't want to wake your parents and we need to talk.'

'OK.'

They rode away from the houses and towards the river. When they passed the last flaming torch he continued into the darkness for another couple of minutes and then stopped. He dismounted, then helped her down. He pointed at a nearby tree.

'We could sit in those boughs. They should hold us.'

'OK. You'll have to help me get up there.'

'Of course, Eleanor,' he smiled, 'I may have been living in the wild, but I haven't forgotten how to be a gentleman.'

'You've been living in the wild?'

'Relax. It's not as scary as it sounds.' He kneeled before her, knotting his hands together. 'Here, put your foot here.'

She did so, and he boosted her up into the branches. Eleanor grabbed hold of the trunk and pulled herself into place. Justin scrambled up alongside her.

They sat there in silence for a moment, and then he said, 'So, are you settled?'

'Yes.'

'Good. I guess you want to know where I've been.'

'Very much.'

'OK. I'll start at the beginning. After you left me at the Greengrove Castle, I couldn't help thinking about how cowardly I had been. You gave me the perfect opportunity to escape from my family, and I couldn't take it . . .'

'I didn't think you were cowardly, Justin. Some people might say it would have been cowardly to run away. You stayed to face your father, even though you knew he would be furious because he'd think you'd betrayed him.'

'I did betray him, Eleanor.'

Eleanor felt scared, worried her boyfriend might have come here to tell her he now supported his father. 'If you want to see it like that . . .'

'Don't worry,' he said quickly, 'I'm not fighting for my father's army now.'

'Are you fighting for someone else?'

'No. Well, maybe for myself. And the truth. My father did beat me, when he came back, and he called me every name under the sun. He said that you were much stronger than me, and he couldn't believe that he'd raised such a weakling. It didn't take me long to realise he was right. But I didn't want to come here and beg you to make me part of your team. There was something I had to do for myself. You remember all those conversations we had when you came to the Greengrove Castle, about what might be out there and how most people are terrified of anything beyond their own community?'

'Yes,' she said, 'of course. I've thought about that a lot.'

'Good. Well, I decided that I wouldn't return to you until I had something important to share. And now I do. I have information.'

'What sort of information?'

'Eleanor, you know how most travellers' tales are fairly average stories, little bits of local folklore and tales of places that aren't really that different from where we come from?'

'Yes.'

'But some are really outlandish and strange and impossible to believe?'

She nodded.

'Well, I'm coming to believe that the strange stories are closer to the truth about what's out there.'

'What have you discovered, Justin?'

'OK. We already know that there are connections between many of the central communities. Maybe your community isn't central geographically, but it's central in terms of influence, with the Castle Seven . . .'

'Five,' Eleanor corrected

'What?'

'There's five of them now.'

'Right. Anyway, I decided rather than go round all these central communities, most of which either have already been visited, or will be visited by my father, I decided to travel further afield, to go beyond the areas that even the most dedicated travellers have visited. And do you know what I found?'

'Ghosts?' asked Eleanor, wide-eyed.

He laughed. 'No. I discovered that this myth that most of us believe, that the whole of England is exactly the same, just isn't true. There are areas out there that are . . . almost impossible to describe. Wildernesses unlike any we have seen. I came to this place . . . the people who lived in the settlements there told me it was once the greatest city in the whole of England . . . and I wanted to go further, but it was impossible alone. It's not just this place that's important – now it's mostly deserted – but there's this building, far into the distance beyond where almost anyone, save a brave few, has travelled, and it rears up from the reeds and mud, a vast, ivy-clad tower called the White Castle, and according to local rumours, inside this building are thousands of books and ancient machinery that is more magical than anything we have in our own age. I think this building may hold the key to all the history we have been desperate to discover. I want to go there, Eleanor, and I want you to go with me. We need to discover our country's secrets. If we do this we could save England from my father and change our future for ever. What do you say?'

Eleanor stared at Justin, struggling to take all this in. 'I think it's an amazing idea. That would be the best thing the Castle Five could possibly achieve, and it will put an end to everything that's happening in our community.'

'What's happening here? Has Basker . . . ?'

'No,' she said. 'It's got nothing to do with your father. This time it's my family who are to blame.'

Eleanor explained to Justin the internal strife that was currently affecting her family and her community. He was sympathetic, and agreed with her that the Castle Five should be involved with the mission. They climbed down from the tree and Justin took Eleanor home, promising her that he would come to the meeting the next day and persuade the Castle Five that this was the perfect solution to all their problems.

Chapter Four

Eleanor awoke to see her father sitting on the edge of her bed. He looked serious, and immediately started apologising. 'I'm so sorry that you've got caught up in the middle of this, Eleanor. I'm afraid I haven't set a very good example to you. I don't know why I've been so stupid. After all, it's not as if I don't understand why April feels the way she does. When you first got chosen to go to the Castle I was intimidated and scared. I consider myself an experienced man . . . I may not have travelled much, compared to some, but I've definitely done a lot of things in my life. And when you started coming home and trying to tell me about all the stuff that you had been taught, I felt jealous and worried that you would think less of me because I didn't know what you were talking about.'

Eleanor sat up. 'I would never have done that.'

He looked ashamed. 'I know that now. I also know that my experiences with the Castle Six, or Five, haven't changed the way I feel about April one bit . . . but I've failed to communicate that to her.'

'Dad, what are you going to do?'

'I'm going to leave the Castle Five for a bit. I need to make that sort of sacrifice to her if she's going to believe I'm sincere about putting her first for a while.'

'Did she give you an ultimatum?'

He looked away. 'It wasn't like that.'

'Listen, Dad, you can't do that. This thing is bigger than you . . . it's bigger than your relationship with Mum . . . and I don't just mean the Castle Five, I'm talking about the future of our entire country.'

'I don't understand . . .'

'OK . . . last night Justin came to the house. You remember the boy from the Greengrove Castle?'

'Yes. Basker's son? He came here? When? In the middle of the night?'

'Yes.'

'And? What? Basker's on the warpath again?'

'Yes. But that's not it. He's discovered something.' She explained to her father everything Justin had told her about the White Castle. 'So, you see, you can't bow out now. Tell Mum this is it, your last mission – then you'll devote all your time to her. She has to understand. If she doesn't, she's just being selfish.'

'I'm not sure it's as simple as that, Eleanor.'

'It is. If you were telling me the truth last night, that

there's nothing between you and Alexandra. Except friendship.'

'Of course I'm telling the truth. I'm your father. I would never lie to you.'

'Then convince Mum you have to do this. And if she can't accept that, well, she can continue her campaign until we return and she realises how stupid she's been.'

'*Eleanor*. That's your mother you're talking about.'

She stared at her father, surprised to hear him defending April, but pleased at the same time.

'I know, Dad. But it's like you told her last night. She has no idea how destructive her actions are. What if the Community really turned against us? If they decided to attack us? To kill us?'

'Eleanor, that's ridiculous. But you're right. This could be an incredible discovery, and I should be part of it. I'll talk to her.'

He left her bedroom and Eleanor smiled to herself, pleased to have persuaded her father to stick with her.

CHAPTER
FIVE

The meeting was supposed to start at five-thirty, but was postponed until seven. When the group finally sat down at the table, Eleanor was so eager to share her news that she started gabbling even before the meeting had started. Alexandra raised her hand. 'I'm aware that you have important things to tell us, Eleanor, but we do have an order of business tonight. In times like these, it's important that we get all the information and everyone has a chance to speak.'

Eleanor sat down reluctantly, knowing that what she had to say was more important than anything anyone else had to share. 'Now,' continued Alexandra, 'Mary, what happened when you went to the "Down With The Castle Five" meeting? Were there many people there?'

'Loads,' Mary said with a sigh. 'And the main person speaking at the meeting was your mum, Eleanor.'

'I know,' Eleanor said, noticing Alexandra look at Jonathan. Surely he had already told her about this?

– 40 –

Alexandra seemed to recover herself and addressed Mary again. 'What are their main grievances?'

'Well, she started off by saying that the Community has been denied a say in things. Then she talked about how Anderson started the group and when he turned out to be evil the group should've been abandoned.'

'There's something to that argument,' noted Zoran.

Alexandra ignored him. 'What else?'

'She told the crowd that the Castle Five doesn't properly represent the Community. She said when you visit another castle you only talk to the top rulers and not the ordinary people. She said that the Clearheart Community is made up of humble individuals and that they would be ashamed if they saw how you were representing them.'

Jonathan started to say something. Alexandra frowned at him. 'Mary, please continue . . .'

'The good news is that they're not going to take any immediate action. April doesn't know who she can get to fight her case . . . but, be warned, she is considering talking to the army or making contact with other communities. She has various strange ideas about how to change the Castle Five, a lottery, an election . . . which they would let you participate in . . .'

'That's absurd,' interrupted Sarah. 'Not just anyone can do our job. Don't they understand? We're diplomats.' She turned on Alexandra. 'I told you it was a bad idea to . . .'

Alexandra raised her hand again, but this time Jonathan ignored her disapproval and asked Sarah, 'A bad idea to what? What were you going to say?'

'Nothing,' she replied.

'No, don't do that. Say what you were going to say. The whole point of this meeting is to get everything out into the open.'

Sarah looked at Alexandra, clearly considering something. 'OK, Jonathan, if you really want to know, I didn't want you to join the group. I knew it was a mistake. If Alexandra hadn't been so keen on the idea . . .'

'But it wasn't just Alexandra who asked me. The two of you came together.' His voice sounded hurt and Eleanor wished she knew how to bring this conversation to an end.

'We did argue,' Alexandra confessed. 'I made her come with me when we talked to you. She was adamant that it was a bad idea, but I won her over.'

'I don't have anything against you, Jonathan,' Sarah explained. 'But I could always foresee this day coming. I didn't realise it would be your wife that would bring it about, but, nevertheless, when we allowed you to join our group it was inevitable that it would eventually lead to dissent from the Community. In order for our group to mean something we have to be different from everyone else. You may be physically blessed and have some startling skills, Jonathan, but, essentially, you're one of them.'

Jonathan didn't respond. Alexandra said, 'Actually, what Sarah is saying is important. But rather than leading to the Castle Five's dissolution, your presence may just salvage the group. So April's stirring everyone up by saying the Castle Five are unrepresentative of the Community, well, how can that be true when you're one of us?'

'And I'm not exactly of noble birth either,' pointed out Zoran.

'Yes,' said Alexandra. 'Jonathan, don't take offence, and Sarah, please try to keep your snobbery in check. We are all aware of your birthright.'

Sarah sat there, quietly fuming. Alexandra noticed this and said, 'If you've got something to share . . .'

'You know, I have an open invitation to go to the Daughters' Community whenever I want to, and yet I stay here, with you, giving you the benefit of that birthright you mock so readily. If you don't value my presence . . .'

Alexandra cut her off. 'Of course we value your presence, but the Castle Five is not in the business of re-establishing old hierarchies. If that's what *you* wish to do, then maybe you should go to the Daughters' Castle.' She paused. Sarah didn't respond. 'But I believe that you are a member of this group because you understand that it is the future that we look to, and this will be a future that is different from our past.

'From what you have said, Mary, it seems the solution to our problem is obvious. If we have a fault, it is one of image. We have, for whatever reason, remained aloof from our community and it is unsurprising that they should regard us with suspicion. If we are to convince them that it is worth continuing to support us, we need to successfully achieve a mission that points out the purpose of our group and why we are valuable to them. So, does anyone have any ideas?'

'The Baldwin Community suggested we should visit them,' said Lucinda.

'No,' said Alexandra, 'there is little to be achieved in that mission, and it would seem as if we were merely returning to the site of one of our former glories. Eleanor – you had an idea?'

Eleanor, who had been very irritated by having to sit through all this bickering, stood up and said, 'It's not an idea, it's the solution. There is this place, some people call it the White Castle, others The Repository, and in this place there are records and papers and information fully detailing the history of England. I understand that you want a future that is different from the past, but surely it will be worthwhile to know what happened before we were here?' She appealed to Sarah. 'To find out how the Kingdom fell?'

Alexandra asked, 'How did you find out about this place, Eleanor?'

'Justin told me about it.'

'Basker's son?' said Lucinda, shocked. 'When did you meet him?'

'He came to me the other night.'

'He's in our community?' demanded Alexandra. 'And this is his idea?'

'Yes. Why does that worry you?'

'Eleanor, isn't it obvious?' asked Sarah, in a patient voice. 'What if he's in league with his father? This whole thing could be an elaborate ruse. He leads us away on some wild-goose chase, then when we're gone his father attacks the Clearheart Community.'

'You don't have to worry about that,' said a voice from the corridor. Eleanor looked up to see Justin stride into the room. 'I haven't even seen my father for months. Anyone from the Greengrove Community could verify that for you.'

The group stared at Justin. Eleanor hadn't known that he'd followed her to the meeting. She hadn't seen him since the night before, and was curious to know where he was staying. Probably camping in the wilderness by the look of him.

'Justin,' said Alexandra, 'this is a private meeting . . .'

'But you're talking about me.'

'You have Eleanor to defend your case . . .'

'But she can't vouch for me, and it's unfair to expect her to do so. I've come back into her life, your lives, out of nowhere. I can understand why you're suspicious of me, and it's better that I answer your questions than she does.'

The room considered this. Zoran asked, 'OK, where is your father?'

'I don't know. Like I said, I haven't seen him.'

'But he wants to attack our Castle and Community?'

'Of course. You humiliated him, and this is an important location if he's ever going to rule England. But I don't know when he might strike, and whether or not you go to the White Castle will make no difference to him. I doubt he's even employing spies. He's too arrogant for that, and he's convinced he has God on his side to guide him.'

Eleanor watched her friend, pleased and impressed that he was holding his own against this tough audience. It hadn't occurred to her that this might be a trap, but as much as she wanted to trust Justin she couldn't help remembering that it was his hands that had shoved her into the oubliette. OK, he had later explained that he had to do it, and playing along with his father's plan was the only way he could trick him into trusting him so that he could help Eleanor escape, but a small part of her would never forget this temporary betrayal.

'If we're honest with ourselves,' asked Jonathan, 'is it really going to make any difference whether we're here when Basker decides to invade? It will be the army that holds his forces back, and unless we decide to quit going on missions altogether and stay here for ever, it's going to happen eventually.'

'Yes,' said Alexandra, 'but you're forgetting the main point of this exercise is public relations. If we go away and the Community is invaded . . .'

'Then maybe they'll value us more,' suggested Sarah. 'Look, I think the boy has a good argument. And it's not as if we have a great deal of choice. If we're searching for a mission that is going to make us look good, then I think this is the best one we're going to get.'

Zoran stood up. 'This is ridiculous . . .'

Everyone turned, surprised by his outburst. It was extremely rare for the laid-back Zoran to express emotion, especially anger.

'Why?' asked Justin.

'You're playing into the Community's hands. Don't you understand how they'll see this? Eleanor's mother has managed to galvanise the people because she's speaking to them in terms they understand. You've been living this life of luxury so long that you've completely forgotten how normal people think. This mission will seem just as pointless to them as everything else we've done . . .'

Justin waited until he had finished, and then said, 'Will they understand riches?'

'What?'

'That wealth will bring you power . . . that if this mission is successful, the Clearheart Community might gain the means to rule the entirety of the former kingdom?'

Jonathan stared at Justin. 'Explain yourself.'

'Gladly. It's not just records and papers and information in the White Castle. There's also the Crown Jewels, riches that used to belong to the former kingdom. Items so valuable that we could ask any price we wanted and still receive it.'

'Then why hasn't someone taken them already?'

'Because it's hard to get to the Castle, and dangerous. People are superstitious.'

'Like at the Kingmaker's Castle,' added Eleanor. 'I think we should go back there and persuade them to come with us. They're probably the only people we know in the whole of England who will be able to decipher even the most arcane information. And with their experience with the System, community history and libraries . . .'

'Justin,' asked Alexandra, 'have you been to the Kingmaker's Castle?'

He shook his head.

'Do you know where it is?'

'Roughly. I've read about it in my father's library.' He looked at Eleanor. 'Without him knowing, of course.'

'And is it in the direction of this . . . White Castle?'

'It can be . . . without too much difficulty. And our journey will be so long that it would do us good to have somewhere to stop along the way.'

'OK,' said Alexandra. 'I'm not going to put this to a vote, as it seems that we're all in broad agreement, but if there is anyone who thinks this is a bad idea, I would like to hear their reasons now.'

The room remained silent.

'Good. We will leave in three days. It will take us that long to prepare for an expedition of this length. In the meantime, I will dispatch a messenger to the Kingmaker's Castle to warn them of our intentions. Justin, I will need a fuller description of this White Castle and what we should expect when we get there. I realise you may not be able to be exact, but I shall be grateful for any intelligence you have gathered. And unless anyone is against the idea, I think we should announce our mission to the Community tomorrow evening. Agreed?'

'We should write up posters as well,' suggested Stefan. 'Fight fire with fire.'

'That's an excellent idea. Zoran, can you help the boy with that?'

Zoran nodded.

'Great. Good evening, everyone. This meeting is concluded.'

Chapter
Six

It was the first time Basker had addressed an audience of wilderness-dwellers. In the months since he had been released from the Clearheart Castle dungeon he had changed his tactics considerably. He'd realised that there was no point in either collaborating with other communities or trying to trick them. His old allies, Anderson and Katharine, now resided in the same dungeon he had once been held in, and he knew that the only way to achieve leadership of the country was through brute force. Unfortunately, the Greengrove Castle army, while twice the size of the Clearheart Castle's army, was smaller than that of many other communities. If he was going to overpower the communities of a significant number of castles, he needed a much larger army, which meant he needed to recruit, and the easiest place to do this was in the wilderness.

There were many different wilderness areas. Most were featureless, forgotten patches, but others had their own folklore and rumours, and the soldiers Basker had sent ahead to find out about these places had reported that while many of the people who lived in the wilderness were dangerous characters who had been cast out from their communities, others took pride in the fact that they had stories and legends that dated back far beyond the time most people who lived in communities could remember. The area they were targeting today was called Tyger Island. Basker and his army had set up camp a short distance away, and he had sent four of his best soldiers to try to find out who was in charge, and whether the dwellers could be gathered together so he could talk to them. When the soldiers returned, they told Basker that a crowd would gather at six o'clock, but they did not look like they would be easy to win over.

Basker stroked his black moustache and stared into the distance. 'Good. When you're recruiting an army, you don't want hundreds of useless people who've signed up just for something to do. The people who are most reluctant to join usually prove to be the most loyal.'

The four soldiers did not reply, and Basker was pleased they were too intimidated to answer back.

At five to six Basker and his soldiers approached Tyger Island. There was a large crowd, bigger than he had expected. But he was sure his voice would carry far into the night air. There was no stage for him to stand on, but Basker's presence was intimidating enough to quieten his audience.

'My name is Basker. I am the leader of the Greengrove Community. I understand that many of you will be disturbed that I have come here to speak to you, and no doubt will struggle to understand when I tell you that I am here to talk about liberty . . . or rather, a fight for liberty. No doubt you believe that you have greater freedom than anyone else who lives in England . . .' He paused, not expecting any dissent, and when none followed, he continued. 'And in a way that is true. But let's be honest here, the reason why you have this freedom is that no one has challenged it. The reason why no one has challenged your freedom is because the country is in an incredible state of disarray . . . but you must know, in your hearts, that things will not continue like this for ever. If I can find you, then others can too. There has never been a time when history provides so little instruction for the present day, but nevertheless, there are lessons to be drawn from the past, when, of course, you look at the broadest sweep of history and you must believe me when I say that we are about to enter a period of profound change. Order will be restored. That is inevitable. The question you have to ask yourselves is, when order is restored, what position do you want to be in? You have opted out of communities, but maybe soon England won't be structured in this way. Maybe one day the entire wilderness will be something of the past. But if you agree to follow me, to fight with me, I can ensure that will not happen.

'Let me make myself clear. I am not asking everyone here to fight. Even if you wanted to, a small proportion of you will not have the stamina necessary for prolonged combat. But if some of you . . . even a small number . . . volunteer to join my army I will give you my personal guarantee that your wilderness will be preserved, your homes will be unharmed, and you will not have to do anything you don't want to . . . This will be a while in the future, and maybe some of the oldest of you won't be around for that, but I know how highly you value your history, and those who fight today will be heroes to your grandchildren.'

Basker stopped, looking at the faces in front of him and waiting for a question. After a moment, someone asked, 'Who will we be fighting against?'

'Well, other castles and communities. But I should explain that this is not a question of attacking normal people . . . you will, the volunteers, I mean . . . be fighting against armies, and the aim is not to indulge in unnecessary violence, but to use force to restore order.'

'And what happens if we don't win?'

Basker noticed the tacit acceptance in this use of the word 'we' and felt a surge of confidence. Not that he'd been nervous, but he had worried that the group might simply hear him out without responding.

'There is no possibility of us not winning, as long as we act now. No one else in England is thinking in this way, and the only possible threat to my leadership is if we are invaded from overseas.'

'But you said the wilderness might be threatened when order is restored. If you're the only person who can restore order, then the only threat to the wilderness comes from you.'

Basker backtracked, aware this could prove dangerous. 'No, the threat comes if someone else succeeds in uniting England, and that can only happen if I fail, and the only reason I might fail is if I don't manage to recruit a powerful enough army.'

This silenced them. Basker took advantage of this moment to say, 'My soldiers are among you. If anyone here wants to join my army, tell them your names and they will advise you where to assemble tomorrow morning. I thank you for your time.'

He walked away from the crowd. Two soldiers approached him and clapped him on the back.

'Well done, sir. I think we will get a fair number of recruits tonight.'

He nodded. 'Yes. They're intelligent too, aren't they? Much more so than our community. Maybe there's something to be said for living in the wilderness.'

The soldier laughed. 'Not that they'll be able to do that for much longer.'

Basker smiled. 'No.'

CHAPTER
SEVEN

Eleanor's parents refused to let Justin sleep at their house. Eleanor could understand why April didn't want him there, as to her, he represented everything she was fighting against, but couldn't see why her father wouldn't let him sleep in their lounge. When she argued with him, he said, 'Eleanor, he seems to have coped fine with sleeping rough up until now. And, who knows, maybe he even prefers being outside. Besides, this is a good way for him to prove himself to us.'

She had no idea what her father meant by this, but so many things had gone her way recently that she was prepared to let this one slide, especially as Justin didn't seem that bothered. When they returned to their house after the meeting, he kissed her goodnight and rode off to find himself somewhere to sleep. Jonathan and Eleanor entered their house. April was lying on the sofa, waiting for them. Eleanor looked at the orange stockings April was wearing and worried that her anger with her mother would never diminish.

'So,' April asked, 'how was your meeting?'

Jonathan sighed. 'We're going to need your help on this one, April.'

She sat up. 'My help?'

'Yes, that's right. We need you to convince people that no matter how they feel about the Castle Five, they have to come to our meeting tomorrow evening.'

'Oh,' she said, 'I'm sorry, that's impossible. No, there's no way I could do that.'

'Why? I thought you said you understood why Eleanor and Justin's plan would be good for the Community?'

'Yes, if it's a success, but there's no guarantee of that, is there?'

Eleanor started to protest.

'Oh, shut up, Eleanor. This boy has bewitched you. Maybe what he says *is* true, but who knows? I'm building up a valuable position in this community, people are starting to trust me, and I can't ruin that with a sudden, inexplicable volte-face.'

'But it wouldn't be inexplicable. You could say that you'd realised the Castle Five do have a point after all.'

She laughed. 'Jonathan, I'm letting you and Eleanor do this because it's important to you, but it doesn't mean I'm going to go back to being the happy little wife indoors. We need to change the way this community is run, and if the Castle Five is to continue holding its prominent position the group has to prove its worth. But I'm not going to tell people I made a mistake.'

Jonathan sat down and started tugging off his boots. 'I'm not asking you to do that. All I'm asking is: can you help get people to this meeting? You'll all get chance to have your say.'

'We'll see,' said April. 'It all depends whether we feel you're trying to co-opt the resistance movement.'

He shook his head and made a face at Eleanor. She put her hand over her mouth, not wanting her mother to hear her giggle.

The public meeting the following evening proved much smaller than everyone had hoped. April had stayed away, and it was impossible to know if any of the thirty who did show up were among those who had gone to her meeting two nights before.

Alexandra and Jonathan addressed the crowd, explaining about the White Castle and what they expected to find there. A few older members of the crowd asked questions, and it seemed obvious that they were more excited about these possible discoveries than the younger people, who, Eleanor deduced from their excitable manner, had come in the hope of witnessing a fight or a serious argument. The Castle Five were deflated at the end of the meeting, but Jonathan attempted to cheer them up by saying, 'They'll change their minds when they see what we bring back from the White Castle. We'll be heroes then.'

'Maybe to the old folk,' said Zoran, 'but I can't see anyone else getting excited unless we discover a recipe for a new-flavour beer.'

'Well, perhaps we will,' replied Justin.

'Really?' asked Zoran, and his eyes were so wide that everyone laughed, aware that for him too this was the most thrilling discovery they could possibly make.

CHAPTER EIGHT

Three days later, the group was ready to go. Breaking with tradition, they breakfasted at the Castle. Everyone was aware that this was the longest, most complicated, and possibly most dangerous mission they had yet attempted, but instead of feeling afraid, most of them were excited about getting back on the road. Travelling was a freedom for everyone, but Eleanor especially was pleased to get away from her home. Jonathan was a different person away from April and now the group was smaller they found they could travel much faster than before. The first day's riding was much harder than usual, and when they stopped to eat a short picnic lunch, Jonathan didn't bother to look for an interesting spot to rest as he normally did, and he warned everyone in the group not to wander off. Their intention was to get to the Kingmaker's Castle in two days, and they arrived at the inn that stood at the midway point of their journey much earlier than they had last time they travelled this way.

A stable-boy appeared to help them with their horses and luggage. When he commented on the amount of stuff they had with them, Hephzi started to explain about their mission. Sarah gave her a stern look and she immediately stopped talking. The stable-boy looked at each of them in turn and then said, 'You don't have to worry about me, but I understand why you don't want me knowing what's happening. You've come here before, haven't you? You're the Castle Six, aren't you?'

'Five now,' said Hephzi.

Eleanor came over and took Hephzi's arm. 'Come on, let's go upstairs and unpack.'

The other children noticed the two of them going and came across, ready for the usual squabble over who would have which bedroom. They went upstairs and Eleanor separated from Hephzi, returning to Justin. Once she had selected a bedroom, she went inside and sat on the bed. A few moments later, Justin entered her room.

'Last time I was here I did a bad thing,' she told him.

'Here?'

'In this inn.'

'Oh. What did you do?'

'Do you promise to keep it secret?'

'Of course.'

'I didn't really know what I was doing until after I'd done it. I don't mean that as an excuse. I'm just telling the truth, that's the way it happened.'

'What happened?' asked Justin, a hint of exasperation in his voice.

'I was having a nightmare and I woke up in the middle of the night. I realised I needed the toilet so I went out into the corridor and I saw Sarah standing in the doorway of her room, tearing up an envelope and a letter. I realise I shouldn't have done this, but you have to understand that Sarah is so enigmatic that we're all desperate to know her secrets.'

'You took the letter.'

'Yes.'

'What did it say?'

Eleanor walked across the room to the desk by the window. Then she looked down at the floor and tried to locate the loose floorboard that she had found before. Spotting it, she knelt down and used her fingernails to tug it up. Although she knew it was unlikely that anyone else would have discovered it, she still felt slightly surprised to find the pieces still there. She put them back together and handed them to Justin.

He looked at the card:

THE DAUGHTERS 225TH ANNIVERSARY
The Daughters' Castle
42nd Week, Day One
Nightfall
R.S.V.P.

'So,' he said, 'Sarah's a Daughter?'

'I think so. I mean, it makes sense. She's the great-great-granddaughter of the last princess before the fall of the kingdom.'

'Yes,' he said, 'I knew that. It was one of the things that surprised me most about the way my father behaved when you came to visit our castle.'

'How d'you mean?'

'Well, OK, he wanted to trick you all and to invade your castle, but even if he'd succeeded, it was strange that he'd choose to further his plans by making connections with Anderson and Katharine. It would have made far more sense for him to have teamed up with Sarah.'

'So your father does want to restore things to the way they were?'

'No, not really, because then he wouldn't have any power at all. But he is always seeking allies, and the Daughters are exactly the sort of people he might speak to, try to convert to his cause and pretend he's acting on their behalf when that isn't true at all. A temporary allegiance.'

'Sarah's not a bad person, is she?'

'No, you saw her tearing up this invitation. And even if she didn't, she's chosen to live in your community instead of with the Daughters, which would be much easier for her.'

'She threatened to go there the other night, during our

meeting. I thought you heard that. I thought you were eavesdropping?'

'No, I could hardly hear what anyone was saying until they mentioned my name.' He smiled. 'After that I made a special effort. But I don't think you need to worry about Sarah. She seems like a good person.'

Eleanor smiled. 'I'm so glad you said that. I couldn't bear it if there was another person I couldn't trust.'

He kissed her. 'Eleanor, I promise I will never let anyone betray you again.'

She smiled. 'That's a silly promise. But thank you for making it.'

'And now there's something I'd like you to do for me.'

'Name it.'

'I want you to tell Sarah that you've read her invitation, and give it back to her.'

'What?' said Eleanor, startled. 'Why?'

'Because it's been preying on your mind, I can tell. I've learnt from my experiences that it's not good to have secrets from the people you're supposed to trust. You told me about that invitation because you wanted me to absolve you, but it's not up to me to do that. You have to ask forgiveness from Sarah.'

Eleanor stared at Justin, astonished that he was asking this of her. He held her gaze, and she nodded meekly, leaving him in her room while she went downstairs to find Sarah. She was standing by the entrance to the bar, rubbing a cloth against her muddy boots.

'Sarah?' said Eleanor.

'Yes?' she replied, looking up.

'I have something of yours,' she told her, handing over the pieces of the invitation.

Sarah looked at the crumpled pieces of card. 'How did you get this?'

'I took it from the bin outside your room last time we stayed here. Don't worry, I hid the pieces under a floor-board. No one else has seen them.'

'I don't understand . . .'

'I'm sorry, I was curious. I wanted to know your secrets.'

Sarah stared at Eleanor. 'I can't believe you did this.'

'I know, I'm sorry, please forgive me.'

'Have you done anything else like this before? Or since?'

She shook her head. 'It was the only time. I'm sorry.'

'Now I understand why you were asking so many questions about the Daughters' Castle.'

'I know. It's none of my business. I was just intrigued. Please don't tell anyone else I did this.'

Sarah didn't say anything for a moment, then she took Eleanor's hands and said, 'Promise me you will never snoop again. On your parents' lives.'

'I promise.'

'Then I forgive you. But if you break your promise I

will have to talk to Alexandra about whether you are of suitable moral calibre to remain in the group.'

Eleanor felt irritated with Sarah for saying this, and cross with Justin for making her apologise, but didn't answer back to her, instead nodding and stepping away. When Sarah turned her back on her, Eleanor ran up to her room, wanting to get ready for the evening meal.

CHAPTER
NINE

Eleanor knew that if the Castle Five was to survive, the group had to regain their old confidence. Tonight the whole group assembled for dinner, and Eleanor felt secretly pleased to witness Zoran and Justin joking with each other. She knew Zoran missed his friend Robert and it made her happy to see him making friends with someone new. She hadn't expected this, assuming Zoran would hold Basker's crimes against his son, but it seemed he had forgiven Justin for his part in getting him imprisoned at the Greengrove Castle.

Hephzi and Michael seemed as happy as ever, sitting together at the end of the table. But Stefan was quieter than usual and Eleanor turned to see how he was feeling.

'It's a lot less lively without Beth, isn't it?' she asked him.

Stefan smiled. 'Yeah.'

Mary looked up at the mention of Beth's name. Eleanor noticed this and said, 'When you went to my mother's meeting together . . .'

'Yeah?'

'Did you get the impression that she'd ever rejoin the group?'

'It depends if the mission is successful, I think.'

'Yeah,' said Hephzi, 'and when it is she's going to feel so stupid. Doing all this just to get some attention.'

Alexandra and Sarah were listening to their conversation, and hearing this, were quick to voice their disapproval. 'We mustn't make it hard for the Community to accept us,' said Alexandra. 'If we've learnt one thing from what's happened it's that we have to let them see our worth without boasting about it. And if Beth sees the error of her ways and wants to rejoin the group we should let her do so without comment.'

'Yes,' said Sarah, looking at Eleanor instead of Hephzi, 'I've realised I was wrong to get so upset about your father joining the group. Alexandra's right . . .' She smiled at her. 'Not about everything, of course, but in this instance, definitely. The old ways won't work any more. We should see this as a test we should've passed ages ago. This is an interesting period for us and a tremendous new strength is going to emerge from our success, but we have to make the Community think they have chosen us. They have to believe we are their appointed leaders.'

'It's going to be exciting, though, isn't it?' asked Hephzi. 'The White Castle.'

'Of course,' laughed Alexandra. 'And the Kingmaker's Castle are going to love hearing about this. Have you met them, Justin?'

He looked up, wiping his mouth with the back of his hand and picking up a piece of bread. 'No. I've heard about them, of course . . .'

'Oh,' said Eleanor, her words coming out in an excited rush, 'they're great. There's four of them. Two women, Hedley and Sophie, and two men, James and Stewart. At first I thought that Sophie was my favourite because we share the same birth-sign. We're both Questers. She's got dark hair and she's the youngest. But then I realised that James is really nice too. The others didn't like him as much because he's not very gregarious and some people might think he's lazy because he spends all his time reading while he pretends that he's thinking about all these mathematical theories. Stewart's more friendly, at least he seems friendly at first, but there's something reserved about him. He's like the opposite of James. With James, he holds you at arm's length at first, but then when you start talking to him he really opens up, while Stewart greets everyone with total excitement and then starts to seem colder as you get to know him. Hedley's not very friendly at all, at least not to me . . .'

'OK, Eleanor,' said Sarah, 'that's enough. Justin doesn't need to know their complete life histories . . .'

Eleanor felt shocked by this rebuke, and didn't say

anything in reply. She knew she was only talking to her like this because of their conversation about the letter, and felt angry with Justin for making her confess. Annoyed about the way they were treating her, Eleanor finished her meal without saying anything more, letting the others take over the conversation.

It was a long meal, and by the time they finished most of the group were ready for bed. But Mary, Hephzi, Michael and Stefan headed to the games room, and Justin suggested to Eleanor that they could go with them.

'No thanks,' said Eleanor. 'I'm going up to bed.'

'Come on,' he said. 'You know you won't be able to sleep.'

'Yes I will,' she replied, 'and even if I can't I'd rather spend some time on my own.'

She walked towards the stairs. He came up behind her. 'What's this about, Eleanor? Are you angry with me?'

'No,' she replied. 'I'm tired.'

'Don't lie to me. You're angry. What have I done?'

'You know what you've done.'

'Is this about the letter?'

Eleanor sighed. 'Yes, OK, it's about the letter. I showed it to you because I wanted you to reassure me that it was OK, not to force me to do something I didn't want to do.'

'Eleanor, I made you do that for a reason.'

'I know. Because you wanted to embarrass me.'

'No, I did it because I want your conscience to be clear. This group is a mess. Everyone is deceiving someone, and after what I've been through with my father I don't want to be part of anything like that any more.'

Eleanor turned away from him. 'Sarah had already told everyone she was a Daughter. It wasn't as if it made any difference whether she knew I'd read the letter or not. Confessing to Sarah has made her angry with me for no reason.'

'You could have refused my request.'

'What?'

'I asked you to tell Sarah what you'd done as a favour to me, you didn't have to do it.'

'Oh, Justin, I'm getting so bored with your mind-games. You're acting all self-righteous, but this is exactly the sort of thing your father would do.'

Considering this the end of the conversation, Eleanor started walking up the stairs, not expecting Justin to respond. When he grabbed her shoulder and yanked her back to face him, she was frightened and looked round to see if anyone else could see them.

'How dare you say that? My father is a power-crazed lunatic. I'm nothing like him . . .'

'Justin, please stop this . . .'

'No. You're coming with me.'

'What? Where?'

'To the stables. Go on.' He pushed her forwards. She didn't want to go to the stables with him, but was afraid to resist. The adults had gone to bed and Mary, Hephzi, Michael and Stefan were too involved in their game to notice them. She walked round the side of the inn to the stables. Justin went inside. She could hear him talking to the stable-boy and considered going back inside the inn. Minutes later, he returned with his horse.

'Get on,' he urged.

'Where are we going?'

'You'll find out. Get on.'

She did as he instructed. Justin slowly led the horse away from the inn and then climbed up in front of her, taking the two of them deep into the darkness.

CHAPTER
TEN

Mary stared at the large wooden pyramid, wondering whether to admit her ignorance. Stefan noticed this and came to her rescue.

'I don't imagine you've played this before, have you?'

She shook her head. 'What is it?'

'Bar Pyramids,' he explained. 'Which is a silly name as there's only one pyramid. What colour do you want to be?'

He held up four coloured balls. She chose the red one. Michael picked the blue ball, Hephzi the yellow, and Stefan was left with the green. He lifted a triangular flap and dropped the balls into the top drawer. He gave the pyramid a spin and then said to Mary, 'Each drawer has a key. Every time you turn the key it opens a hole in one of the sides of the drawer, or at the bottom. There's an intricate system within the pyramid and as each drawer is opened one of the balls runs round the tracks inside until it reaches an impediment. You have to listen carefully to work out where the balls are, but the aim of the game is for your ball to be the last one to drop out of the pyramid.'

'So you're trying to stop your ball getting to the bottom?'

'Theoretically, yes. But the only time you know where your ball actually is is when it runs into one of these open-topped drawers. There's one on each level, but there's no guarantee that your ball will run through these drawers on its way to the bottom.'

'Tell her about the rotation rule,' said Michael.

'Oh yeah,' he said, 'each player is allowed to turn the pyramid onto a different side once in the game. The reason for doing this is if you see your ball in the open-topped drawer on the bottom level, you can put it back up to somewhere near the top. But the rotation shifts the order of all the drawers and you might find this is no help at all. Or, if you want, you can rotate the pyramid at a random moment, to stop the other players coming up with a strategy. Although as almost all of the game takes place within hidden drawers it's hard to work out what's going on, and only the most experienced players have any real sense of what happens inside the pyramid.'

'This sounds extraordinarily complicated,' said Mary.

'It is,' said Hephzi, 'but the games are surprisingly simple. Sometimes they go on for hours, if everyone keeps rotating at the right minute, but most games we've played have been over really quickly.'

'OK,' said Stefan, 'we take our first turns in the order

of our names in the alphabet. So Hephzi goes first.'

Mary watched as Hephzi turned a key in the middle of the pyramid.

'But no balls are down there, surely?' said Mary.

'That's the reason for her move. That's why the games can go on for a long time, but usually somebody gets things rolling . . . so to speak . . . fairly quickly.'

Mary looked at Michael. 'You next,' he told her.

Wanting to be brave, she turned the key in the first drawer, hearing a ball drop down what sounded like two levels. 'Is there only ever one ball in each drawer at any time?' she asked Stefan.

'Apart from the top one, obviously. And next time someone turns a key in the top drawer, another ball will go in a different direction.'

'I like this game,' said Mary. 'It's tense without being too vindictive.'

Stefan smiled. 'Me too.'

Michael stepped up and turned the first drawer key again, then squatted beside the pyramid, listening.

Stefan laughed. 'You can't hear where they are.'

'Yes I can,' Michael protested, pointing at a drawer. 'My ball's in that one.'

Everyone found this funny. As the game continued, the first moment of tension occurred when Hephzi's ball appeared in one of the open-topped drawers towards the bottom of the pyramid.

'Oh no,' she said, 'I'm almost out.'

'Yeah, but you don't know where the other balls are. They could be lower, or maybe if you turn the right key someone else's ball might drop out. But the obvious strategy is to do a rotation. In fact,' he goaded her, 'you'd be an idiot not to.'

'Yes, OK, Stefan, I have played it before.'

Mary looked up, but quickly decided she hadn't intended any offence. Hephzi stepped forward. Mary knew Stefan had been telling Hephzi to do a rotation so she wouldn't do one just to spite him and risk losing the game, but she also knew that Hephzi wouldn't fall for this. At least that's what she thought until Hephzi took a deep sigh and turned a key. There was a long series of clicks and thuds and then, to everyone's amazement Stefan's green ball rolled out of the bottom of the pyramid.

'You bitch,' he said, although there was no anger in his voice, 'how did you do that?'

'Pure luck. Besides, I'm sure I'll also be out in a minute.'

It was Mary's turn. She rotated the pyramid.

'Why did you do that?' demanded Stefan. 'You're giving Hephzi the advantage. And you've wasted your rotation.'

'How do you know? You said it was hard to predict where the balls would go.'

'Yeah, but look, Hephzi's is still there, in the open-topped drawer at the top.'

'Maybe she's less competitive than you, Stefan,' said Hephzi.

'Oh, that's stupid,' he replied, 'if you're not going to play properly.'

Hephzi winked at Mary, and she could tell she was pleased that they were annoying Stefan. He said, in an irritated voice, 'It's going to take ages if you play like this. I'm going to bed.'

'Goodnight,' said Michael, who waited until Stefan had started walking up the stairs, and then came forward and reversed Mary's move with his own rotation.

'Oh,' said Hephzi, 'that's not fair.'

She tried another key, but it didn't work the same magic, and there was hardly any noise inside the pyramid. Mary stepped up, and wanting to surprise the others, turned the key of the open-topped drawer where Hephzi's yellow ball sat. It rolled out of the pyramid and onto the floor.

'Mean,' said Hephzi. 'You two are doing some sort of trick where you gang up on me.'

'No we're not,' said Michael.

'Sorry,' said Mary. 'I helped you once.'

Hephzi snorted her disapproval and followed Stefan upstairs. Michael and Mary were left together, facing the pyramid.

'Did Beth play this game with you last time you were here?'

Michael looked up. 'Yes, last time we were here.'

'What about Eleanor?'

'She played too. You can put as many balls in the pyramid as you want. In fact, we played one game where we all had two balls each, but it got too complicated.' He contemplated the pyramid. 'I've got no idea where either of our balls is. This bit of the game is more difficult when there's only two of you . . . it can go on for ages if you're not lucky.' He turned a key. Nothing happened. 'Why did you ask me about Beth?'

'No reason.'

'You liked her, didn't you? When you went to that meeting together.'

'What makes you say that?'

'I can tell. You're similar, in lots of ways.'

'What does that mean?'

'It wasn't an insult. I like her too. I'm sad that she's angry with me. But she's wrong to believe that Hephzi stole me. Even if I had been interested in Beth, when I wasn't. It's strange that someone who's a twin would think that way.'

Mary stepped up to the pyramid. She was surprised by the calm, intelligent way Michael was talking to her. From the way Beth had described him she had assumed he wouldn't know his own mind. She turned a key and Michael's blue ball rolled into one of the open-topped drawers midway down.

'What do you mean?' she asked.

'Well, the way she acts is as if they were almost interchangeable. She seems to think that it doesn't matter which twin I go out with, so it might as well be her. Whereas the truth is, I love Hephzi for who she is, not what she looks like. And they may be almost identical to look at, but they're totally different people.' He turned a key, and Mary's ball rolled somewhere different inside the pyramid. 'OK, so I located your ball for a moment, but now I've lost it again. But it's fun, isn't it? We've both had our rotations, it's down to who turns the right key, at the right moment.'

Mary turned the key to the open-topped drawer. His ball disappeared again. She faced Michael and asked, 'Did you tell her this?'

'Beth? Tell her what?'

'The reason for why you feel the way you do about Hephzi, and don't have any feelings for her?'

He considered this. 'Maybe not.'

'Why?'

'Mary, I don't mean to patronise you, but all this is a fairly new experience for you so you're only just beginning to understand how things change. But I used to be this fat, nervous kid who had hardly even talked to a girl. And then everything changed. I lost weight, went through experiences that no one in my community can possibly understand, and suddenly all my anxiety was gone. The idea that both Hephzi and Beth were in love with me, well, it went to my head, and I didn't want either one of them to stop having those feelings for me. Even though Hephzi's the only one I love. Does that make sense? I like it when people like me.'

Mary thought about this. 'I understand that, Michael, but it's caused a lot of trouble. When we get back I think you need to have a long conversation with Beth and be completely honest with her. If you tell her the truth, you won't get in trouble, and she won't tell her sister.'

Michael didn't reply. Instead he stepped up, went for a key that changed nothing, and sighed. 'I think you've got me now.'

His prediction was correct. The next key Mary turned released his ball and it rolled all the way to the bottom. He grabbed it and tossed it into the air.

'Congratulations, Mary,' he said. 'You played well.'

'Beginner's luck.' She smiled, and they went upstairs to their bedrooms.

CHAPTER
ELEVEN

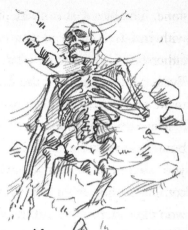

They rode for ages.
Eleanor felt scared, having no idea
where Justin was taking her. All she knew was that he was
trying to prove he wasn't like his father, so she didn't
understand why she was afraid that he might be taking
her to Basker. It was an illogical fear, but one that had
been fed by her nightmares. She had far more nice
dreams about Justin than bad ones, but when she did
have a nightmare it usually involved him turning on her
in some way: even, in one case, actually metamorphosing
into his father. The first dream she'd ever had about
Justin, before meeting him, had started as a happy
dream, as she'd pictured herself dancing with Justin in a
large banqueting hall. But then it had turned into a
nightmare and she'd imagined herself locked in a dungeon. Previously Eleanor had believed this dream was a
premonition of what happened later at the Greengrove
Castle when he tricked her into the oubliette, but now

she remembered that there had been an even more frightening moment at the end of the dream when, trapped in a dungeon, she had crawled across the mouldy straw and then felt her hand touch something hard and brittle, which had turned out to be a skeleton. Before she had gone on her first mission, Eleanor's greatest fears had been wolves and skeletons. Anderson had told her sooner or later she would have to face all her fears, and on that first mission she had been confronted with a wolf. After that showdown she had almost forgotten about her fear of skeletons. It seemed a babyish anxiety. What possible situation could she find herself in where she would have to confront a skeleton? And not just the ordinary bones of a dead body: bones that had been magically bewitched in some way to make them come to life? But what if the skeleton in her dream wasn't something she would literally have to fight, but a symbol of something else? Death was the obvious interpretation, and she wondered if her imagination's nocturnal connection was meant to warn her that Justin would be responsible for leading her to her death, and she shuddered.

'We're nearly there,' he shouted to her as he started to slow down.

'Where?' she asked.

'A wilderness spot called Tyger Island.'

'The wilderness?' she said, scared.

'Yes, but don't worry, I won't let anything happen to you.'

Eleanor had ridden through wilderness spots several times before, but she had never stopped long enough to meet the people who lived there. She knew they were supposed to be frightening, unruly people, individuals who couldn't cope with their communities. Why would Justin want to interact with them?

He stopped, and they both got down from the horse. Holding him by his reins, Justin led the horse alongside them as they approached the first shack. There was a small group of people sitting around a fire.

'Hello,' shouted Justin.

They all looked up, but didn't reply or move. Justin came closer. 'My name is Justin, and this is Eleanor. Can I ask you a question?'

An old man looked over at him. 'It's still a free country.'

Another figure laughed. 'Or so they tell us.'

'OK. Has Basker been here?'

Eleanor noticed that the man's voice had changed as he called back. 'What do you know of Basker?'

'I'm his son. My name's Justin.'

There was an uneasy moment, before the man asked, 'What do you want with us?'

'Nothing. I just want to know, has he been here?'

One of the figures by the fire said to the old man, 'No man knows the father save the son.'

'True,' said the old man. He turned to Justin. 'But are you here as a soldier?'

He shook his head. 'I haven't seen my father in some time.'

The group talked to each other in hushed voices for a moment and then the old man said, 'We have no loyalty to Basker. Yes, he has been here. He is recruiting for his army.'

Justin looked at Eleanor. 'Do you know where he's going next?'

The old man sighed. 'Of course not. He came here to collect men, that's all.'

'How many went with him?'

'Many. That's why it's so quiet.'

'OK,' he said, 'thank you for your time.'

The old man waved a hand. They walked out of earshot of the group and Eleanor asked, 'Why did you bring me here?'

'Because I wanted to prove to you just how serious a danger my father represents. And I wanted you to know, once and for all, that I'm not in league with him.'

Eleanor replied, in a quiet voice, 'I know that, because I trust you. Not because you brought me here. This doesn't prove anything.' She could see Justin was angry. But she wanted to be honest, even if it upset him. 'It doesn't, Justin, surely you can see that? I have to believe you when you say that you're not in contact with your father, that you haven't seen him in a long time, and I do believe you. But you can't prove it until I see you fight him.'

'Is that what you want?' he said with a sneer. 'To see me fight my father?'

'No. I hope we never see him again. But that's not going to happen, is it? As long as he's a force that continues to rise, it's not going to be over until he's crushed.'

Eleanor felt surprised to hear these words coming out of her mouth. She had barely thought about Basker since he was released from the Clearheart Community dungeon after his failed invasion, and whenever anyone else talked about him she couldn't take their rhetoric seriously, thinking 'You haven't faced him. I have, and I'm not afraid.' She knew he saw himself as a dignified figure, a politician, and for this reason she believed he would never be as big a threat to England as some people believed he was. As long as Basker had to invade castles one at a time, there was always the possibility that other communities could bond together against him. And just as the Clearheart Castle had business dealings with the three closest castles (they no longer dealt with Greengrove, of course, but still had connections with the Kingmaker's Castle, Adam's Castle and the Gilbert Castle, and now that Robert ran the Kinder Castle, they had connections with that peculiar community too), so, Eleanor was certain, other castles would have their own links to nearby castles, meaning that there would always be someone to protect all but the most isolated communities. But if Basker was recruiting from the wilderness, then maybe his army would grow to such strength that banding together would make no difference and he would be more successful than he had proved in the past.

'I agree with you, Eleanor. But we cannot win this war through force alone. The people from the wilderness, and from every community will only fight for Basker if they believe he can bring them a better life. You know, the truth is that maybe I am like my father, but only in one way. I want things to change. England is unstable, and instability is dangerous. If the White Castle is as important as I think it is, if the information is useful, if . . . and how I hope this is true . . . the whole history of England up until the fall of the kingdom is recorded there . . . then we could change the country for ever, and for the good. I'm not saying you and I should rule, I don't have those kinds of ambitions, but if we could convince people of the positive force of knowledge . . .'

Eleanor laughed.

'What?' he asked.

'Nothing. You just sound like the people from the Kingmaker's Castle. Especially James. You'll really like him. He told me that we're living through a fascinating period in history because there's no way England can stay the way it is for much longer. He said that the fall of the kingdom came at the end of a long period of decentralisation and that what everyone who predicted it failed to realise was that this Dark Age would be temporary, and it is inevitable that order will be restored.'

'This James sounds like a very intelligent man.'

'He is. They all are, in different ways. But I think James will be the quickest to understand why this discovery could be so important.'

Justin nodded. 'We will need help, if we are going to disseminate this information to everyone in England before my father reaches a position of unassailable power.'

'We're going to do this, Justin. We're going to save England.'

He kissed her. 'I know.'

'But I'm tired now,' she told him. 'Can we go back to the inn, please?'

'Of course.'

Chapter
Twelve

They breakfasted at six a.m., the earliest the inn would serve them. Eleanor had a hard-boiled egg and a bowl of fruit. While the others were finishing their food she went out to the stables with Hephzi.

'What's wrong?' she asked her.

'I don't know which horse is mine. I got a bit confused yesterday, but now I definitely can't tell.'

'What are you talking about, Hephzi? Your horse is white and Nathaniel is grey.'

'They're both white.'

Eleanor went across and looked at the horses, amazed to see Hephzi was right. She hadn't ridden Nathaniel as much as usual when they were back at the Clearheart Community and she'd been so tired after the early start yesterday that she'd barely noticed the change, but it seemed that Nathaniel's colour had definitely changed from grey to white. When she looked more closely at him though she noticed there were still small patches of grey and said to Hephzi, 'This is my horse.'

He whinnied.

'Aw,' she said, stroking him, 'as if I wouldn't recognise you.'

The others were starting to come into the stables behind them. Eleanor stroked Nathaniel and had a disturbing thought. When she had first been given Nathaniel she had complained because in her dreams she had always pictured herself riding a white horse. Although Anderson insisted she rode Nathaniel, when the others were trapped in the Greengrove Community dungeon and she had to ride back to her Castle to get help, she had gone on Hephzibah's horse, which she'd believed fulfilled her premonitions. But now she realised these visions had been of a future date, and the horse she pictured was Nathaniel, after his change. The reason why this disturbed her was that if this dream had now come true in this way, it confirmed that her early visions weren't about the Greengrove Castle mission, but this adventure now, which made her all the more convinced that she would face some form of skeletons, or the death they represented, when they reached the White Castle.

'Are you OK, Eleanor?' asked Hephzi.

'Yeah,' she replied, 'I'm fine.'

Their intention was to get to the Kingmaker's Castle by nightfall. This would entail another day of heavy riding, and only the briefest stop for lunch. In spite of complaints from almost everyone in the group (except Eleanor, who was always cast in a trance by this sort of speed), they succeeded in their aims and arrived at the Castle by seven o'clock.

Sophie and Stewart were waiting for them.

'Hello,' called Sophie, 'hello. We got your message, but it was all very cryptic. What is this all about?'

'We need to talk to you all together,' said Alexandra.

'OK,' said Sophie, 'the others are waiting for you in the dining-room. You remember where it is, don't you? Next to the main hall? Although of course you'll want to go to the stables first.'

Eleanor walked alongside Sophie as they made their way to the dining-room. Mary was also with them and Eleanor said to Sophie, 'This is my friend Mary.'

'Oh,' she said, 'I've heard all about you. You're the one who was kidnapped by Anderson, right?'

Mary nodded.

'It seems extraordinary to me that he's changed like this. When he first came to visit us at the Kingmaker's Castle – this was some time ago – he seemed such a serious, moral man. I haven't met Katharine, but I suppose it must be all her fault. She's probably changed him, right?'

'He is serious,' protested Mary, 'and he has very strict morals.'

'But what about what he did to you? You can't still like him after that, surely?'

Eleanor noticed Mary give her a long look before saying, in a thoughtful voice, 'He wasn't trying to hurt me. It happened because of something Eleanor did, and we've talked about since and it's fine . . .'

'What did you do, Eleanor?' Sophie asked her.

'I betrayed Mary's trust. When we went on our first mission, to the Greengrove Castle, I told Anderson that Mary had a crush on him. He pretended he wasn't interested, and made me feel bad about telling him, but it obviously stuck in his head and that's why he kidnapped Mary . . . because he was trying to recruit her to his cause . . .'

Mary looked at Sophie. 'But you're right, in a way. Katharine has a very different attitude to warfare and politics than Anderson. She's the one who encourages him to violent action, and not just where it's necessary.'

'I don't believe violence is ever necessary,' said Sophie, 'and it shocks me to talk to a child who thinks it is.'

'I'm not a child,' Mary replied in a cross voice, 'and I'm sure I've already had more experience with violence than you have.'

Eleanor felt anxious at this confrontation, and quickly tried to smooth things over. 'I'm sure Sophie didn't mean to insult you, Mary, and it sounds like we should agree to disagree on this issue.'

Sophie didn't reply.

Chapter
Thirteen

James and Hedley stood up as the group entered the dining-room. Eleanor was pleased to see James smile when he noticed her. She'd missed this eccentric man, and hoped he felt the same way about her. What Eleanor liked most about James was his total lack of interest in anything other than the life of the mind. He was wearing his black cloak, which had food splattered on the sleeves, and his glasses were so dirty you could barely see his eyes behind them.

After greetings had been exchanged, they sat down and bowls quickly appeared in front of them, deposited there by the serving staff. It was the same gluey green and brown stew that they'd had last time they came there and Mary whispered to Eleanor, 'Katharine eats this all the time.'

Eleanor nodded, not really interested.

'So,' said James, 'tell us everything.'

Alexandra pointed at Justin. 'He's the one who knows all the details.'

Justin stood up and told the quartet all about the White Castle. Eleanor watched them, amused by the way that Hedley was trying to hide her excitement while the others were openly delighted.

'Do you realise what this means?' James said, when he'd finished. 'This could be the most important discovery since the fall of the kingdom. I've dreamed about something like this happening.'

'The really important thing is how we disseminate this information,' said Sophie. 'It could be dangerous if it's used in the wrong way.'

'I agree,' said Justin. 'This is why we've come to you.'

'OK. Let's work this out. What's the nearest community to this White Castle?'

'I don't know. There might not be any castles there. Most of it is a bigger wilderness than I have ever seen anywhere. But they say it was once the greatest city in the whole of England.'

'Well,' said Hedley, 'that's a matter of opinion.'

'It's called London,' explained James. 'At least, it used to be . . . a long time ago. It used to be the capital city. It's where the kingdom was, once, but not right up until the fall, and it was a centre for finance, society and business. But people haven't lived there for a long time. Now it's a vast, stagnant swamp filled with strange lights and fatal airs, a place which only the crazy and the terminally nostalgic risk visiting. It's one of the dark places of the

Earth, and if we go there it's going to be extremely dangerous for all of us.'

Eleanor was dismayed by his words. 'But you're still excited by this discovery, aren't you, James?'

'Of course! Everything I said before still holds. I just want everyone to be aware of the dangers.'

Sarah cleared her throat. 'With all due respect, James, have you actually been to London?'

He shook his head. 'Have you?'

'Not personally, but I know the Daughters have done some exploratory visits, and while it is true that much of the former city remains extremely treacherous, there are areas that are not like that.'

'Do you know which areas?'

'No,' she admitted, 'but if we go to the Daughters' Castle, I'm sure they would be delighted to share their knowledge with us.'

Sophie laughed. 'We might as well go straight to Basker and tell him what we've discovered.'

'The Daughters' Castle doesn't have any connection with Basker,' protested Sarah.

'My sources at the Sisters' Castle say he does.'

Sarah turned to Justin. 'This is Basker's son. He can tell us. Does your father have any dealings with the Daughters' Castle?'

'I have no knowledge of my father's recent allegiances. I haven't seen him in some time. But as I said to Eleanor when she asked me this question, it would make sense for him to form a temporary connection with the Daughters' Castle.'

Sarah looked exasperated. 'Well, if that's what you choose to believe then we cannot ask them for help. We will have to take our chances.'

'There are ways of minimising danger,' said Stewart. 'There is a guidebook in our library which gives some sense of what we might expect when we get into the abandoned city. Aside from that text, we have no information on what the city might be like now. But we do have thousands of books about what London used to be like . . . maps, guidebooks, first-hand accounts . . . If we combine this knowledge with any information we can gain from people in the wilderness there, then we'll be about as prepared as you can be to enter the unknown.'

'Do we have time for this?' asked Eleanor.

'It will take us a day to prepare for a mission of this nature. In this time, James and Hedley can prepare a lecture for the rest of us. Then we can leave tomorrow night. Agreed?'

There was a murmur of approval.

'Good. Now let's save all further discussion until after we have eaten.'

The following morning, Sarah had gone. This threw everyone into a panic and they assembled in the hall for an emergency meeting.

'This makes things extremely difficult,' said Sophie. 'We now have a time factor that didn't exist before. If Sarah has gone to the Daughters' Castle, which seems the only logical assumption, then Basker is going to know about the White Castle and we have to get there before him.'

'They might not tell Basker,' said Justin. 'They might want to check it out for themselves first.'

'Either way, we have to beat them. And that's going to be almost impossible if they already know the terrain of London. Our only hope is to leave now and travel as quickly as possible.'

'But we're not ready for a mission of this scale,' said Stewart. 'And what are we going to do with the contents of the White Castle? If we can't move it somewhere else, then even if we get there before the Daughters and Basker we'll only have a brief moment to look at the information before they arrive and take it from us. We won't win in a battle. He has a huge army at his disposal, and it's growing every day.'

'We will have to befriend some wilderness-dwellers and get them to help us. It's the only solution. And we will have to be ready to leave in a couple of hours. We will take only minimal supplies. The Castle Five are fully equipped . . . we will rely on them. That's OK, isn't it, Jonathan?'

'Of course. Sarah has only taken her horse. We have her provisions. And we've packed plenty of stuff. We're prepared for anything.'

'What about our training on what to expect when we get to London?' asked Eleanor.

Stewart tossed her the transcribed guide book. 'Read as much of this as you can while we're getting ready. You can tell the others what you've discovered while we ride.'

Eleanor went with James to his tower and he let her recline on the red leather chaise-longue where he did his reading. On the title page she saw the number 1885, but had no idea how that date related to the year she was in now. In school she had been taught that they used to measure time from Anno Domini, the year of the Christian era, but that had long since been abandoned in favour of new dating systems. The weeks remained the same, although no one measured time in months any more. Some people dated years from the fall of the kingdom, but there were arguments about exactly how long ago that had been and most people only really cared about how many years they had been alive. Only in the Kingmaker's Castle was there any real sense of history, and even there, the quartet were frustrated by the gaps in their knowledge, blanks that they prayed might be filled in by the information stored in the White Castle.

When she started reading the book she found the prose incredibly accessible, much easier to follow than *King John*, the Shakespeare play that James had given her to read last time she had been here. She supposed it was easier because the author wasn't trying to invent characters or a story, but just giving a description of the world as he saw it. She remembered James telling her to write an account of her life and supposed this was the sort of thing he wanted her to compose. She felt an immediate empathy with the author and wondered if she would be capable of writing a book like this. She also wondered if the author was still alive. It occurred to her that no one in the Kingmaker's Castle could have read this book properly, because it wasn't really a guide and there was much less information in it about the former city than they had claimed. There was a lot of stuff about rivers, about how the Thames used to flow through the city, but then debris had blocked the waters and the rising of the river destroyed the metropolis. This created the stagnant swamp James had talked about, although the author was even more melodramatic, writing that death would be inevitable for anyone who entered the city. One of the reasons for this, according to the writer, was a 'fatal vapour' that no human could endure. But as she read on, the author relaxed his warnings. Eleanor was pleased to read that if the visitor entered in winter, or at the height of a drought, it would be safe, as long as they didn't break the ice or move anything. She guessed the book must have been written in one of those years past she had read about when winter meant snow and ice, because now although it was the forty-fifth week and technically winter, the weather remained mild. But maybe within London, as the descriptions suggested, the atmosphere would be different. Next he suggested that if the visitor got into London and out within the same day, they might get sick, but it wouldn't be fatal. Then she read that the swamps only took up a portion of London, and even then the outside parts were much less dangerous. Reading carefully, she realised that, with caution and the correct advice, this journey could be completed successfully.

Eleanor heard someone coming up the stairs to James's tower and looked up. It was Stefan. He seemed upset.

'Yes?' asked James, in a stern voice.

'Can I speak to Eleanor?'

'This really isn't the best time.'

'It's OK,' she said. 'I think I've gleaned everything I can from this book. What's wrong, Stefan?'

'Can we talk in private?'

'Well, I'm not leaving,' said James.

'It's OK,' said Eleanor. 'Stefan, let's go outside.'

They did so. Stefan's face was pale and he looked near to tears.

'What's wrong, Stefan?'

'I'm scared, Eleanor.'

'That's OK, Stefan. We're all scared at some point. Michael used to get really frightened before we reached a castle.'

'Yeah, but I'm the one who gets hurt.'

'What d'you mean?'

'When we went to the Greengrove Castle, I was the one who got bitten by the wolf. And I just know it's me who's going to get hurt this time too.'

'The wolf was a random attack. It could've been anyone.'

'Yes, I know, but it was me. Anyway, I'm not asking you for reassurance. What I want to know is, have you had any dreams about this mission?'

Eleanor considered her answer to this question carefully.

The dream about skeletons hadn't been specifically about this mission. So she didn't feel dishonest when she told him, 'Nothing significant. I promise you, you're not in danger. But you mustn't believe you are, because then you'll get all anxious and something bad will happen. You have to be brave, Stefan, OK? For all our sakes.'

He nodded. 'As long as you haven't seen something specific, I'm not afraid.'

She smiled. 'Good.'

CHAPTER FIFTEEN

Two hours later, the group rode out. It took them a while to establish a rhythm, as they now had several leaders. Eleanor could tell her father was happy to stand back and let the Kingmaker's Quartet take charge, but all four of them had different ideas on how best to proceed.

'Look,' said Hedley eventually, in an exasperated voice, 'we shouldn't structure this journey around inns or other communities. Our only concern has to be getting to London as quickly as possible.'

'Yes,' replied Sophie, 'but we can't risk any one of us . . . or the horses . . . getting sick. If we are forced to slow down, we will have failed.'

'If anyone gets sick, they will be directed to the nearest inn and left behind. In a group this size, there will inevitably be problems, but that cannot stop us. Agreed?'

Although Eleanor was troubled by Hedley's harsh words, she could see the wisdom in what she was saying. She thought that because Hedley had an off-hand, harsh manner, and a beauty that was more intimidating than Sophie's or that of any of the Clearheart women, she seemed more combative than she really was. Her suggestions made sense, this was the only way the mission could succeed. And if Eleanor was the one who fell ill and had to be abandoned, she would understand.

'We've started late today,' Hedley continued, 'so we should ride late into the night. We'll stop when we really can't go any further, then take it slower for the next few days. The journey will seem much easier when we've covered an initial distance. It should take us two and a half weeks to get there. Tonight we'll camp out, and unless we happen to pass an inn when we're getting ready to stop on other nights, we'll spend the majority of the journey camping all the way.'

Now that Hedley had taken command, it became easier to plot their journey, and the path was straightforward. Several times during the day Eleanor could feel Nathaniel getting tired beneath her, but he continued without complaint. She whispered to him that after tomorrow they would go slower, and in her heart she believed he understood.

CHAPTER
SIXTEEN

The next fortnight was hard. No one fell sick, but there were times when the horses were exhausted and they had to take a break. They also ended up staying at inns more times than Hedley had predicted, as they frequently arrived at one when they were getting ready to stop, and she could usually be persuaded to trade a night on hard ground for a comfortable bed. The first time they stopped in an inn, Hedley gathered everyone together and gave them a warning.

'This is important for everyone, but I'm addressing it particularly to you, Zoran, as I know how much you like to get away from the group and drink with strangers in the bar.' Zoran looked outraged at being singled out, and grumbled to himself. Hedley ignored him. 'No one can know where we're going. We already have to outrace Sarah, Basker and the Daughters, we don't need any more competition. You cannot say anything to anyone, understood? Don't even talk about the mission among yourselves. It doesn't matter whether you think you are alone and no one can hear you. Absolute discretion, OK?'

They nodded. Eleanor, Mary, Hephzi, Stefan and Michael played a lot of games of Bar Pyramids over those nights, and although everyone got very frustrated about each outcome, the random nature of the game meant there was no obvious champion. This only made the hunger to play all the more keen, and in the quieter moments of the journey, they discussed the game and made jokes about the moves each of them had made on previous evenings. Justin was completely uninterested in the game, and spent most nights alongside James and Zoran, fascinated by their conversation. Eleanor was amazed by how much James had grown to like Zoran, mainly she believed, because Zoran was happy to let James talk about anything while he sat drinking beer. He soaked up knowledge like he did alcohol, and when he did ask questions, Justin reported to Eleanor, they were always incredibly pertinent.

'Zoran's an intelligent man,' Eleanor told Justin, irritated by the way he was patronising him.

'I know,' he said, 'but he drinks so much and acts the goat so often that it comes as a real surprise to hear him being so thoughtful.'

'I'm just glad the three of you get along so well,' said Eleanor. 'Zoran's been really unhappy since Robert left.'

✕

Eleanor, Hephzi and Mary also had a number of long conversations about Sarah, and how they felt about her betrayal. Hephzi had no sympathy for her, claiming she was even worse than Beth (which made Mary flinch), but the other two girls had more ambivalent feelings about her behaviour. Eleanor had always considered Sarah an incredibly sophisticated person, and was reluctant to give up her idealised view of her.

One week into their journey, Eleanor was going upstairs to her room in the inn they were staying at that night when she overheard her father talking to Alexandra at the end of the corridor. He was asking her advice on what to do about April, and saying, 'I can't work out whether she really means what she's saying or if it is just jealousy.'

'Either way,' Eleanor heard Alexandra reply, 'you need to put your foot down.'

'I know,' he replied, 'it's just so hard.'

Embarrassed by her eavesdropping, Eleanor continued up to the landing. When Jonathan saw her, he said goodnight to Alexandra and returned to his room.

Eleanor knew they were getting closer to London when there were no more inns and the wilderness grew thicker and thicker. Everyone was tired now, and arguments were frequent. Eleanor noticed that the group had split into separate units, and people increasingly stuck with their friends. Only Lucinda remained good-natured with everyone, and Eleanor increasingly sought her out when she felt in need of comfort.

'How come you're always so happy?' she asked her one evening.

Lucinda smiled and looked up at the moon. 'Because whenever I feel tired or hungry or sad, I always remind myself of what my life used to be like before I came to the Clearheart Community.'

'When you worked at the inn?'

She nodded.

'But the innkeeper seemed such a nice man.'

'Yes,' said Lucinda, 'he is. But my life there was terrible. Worse than you could possibly imagine. I used to think I would go to my grave without accomplishing anything. Now I've been given a second chance, even if I died on this mission, I would think it worthwhile. Not many people get the opportunity to change their world, Eleanor.'

'I know,' she said. 'I do understand that, and I am grateful.'

'I realise that, Eleanor. You are a very wise person.'

'Thanks, Lucinda,' she replied, hugging her. 'This would be impossible if you weren't here.'

Lucinda didn't reply, but returned Eleanor's embrace and they stayed like that for a moment, before breaking apart. That night, when Eleanor went to bed, she prayed that Lucinda would lead a long and happy life. And although Eleanor had no way of knowing this, Lucinda returned the prayer with a very similar one of her own.

CHAPTER SEVENTEEN

When they reached the outskirts of London, Alexandra took charge. Hedley didn't complain, and seemed relieved that someone else was accepting the responsibility of organising the group. Eleanor knew she still felt guilty about Sarah's betrayal, and wanted to prove herself to the Kingmaker's Quartet.

'Justin,' Alexandra said, 'do you recognise where we are now?'

He nodded.

'Which settlement did you visit last time you were here?'

'One called Handforth Grove. It's about twenty minutes in that direction.' He pointed north.

'Will the people there recognise you?'

'I don't know. I don't think so. I just talked to some people who happened to be walking around that area. I didn't go into anyone's shelter.'

'OK,' she said. 'Everyone gather round.' They did so.

'This is your last opportunity to turn back. In fact, you don't even have to turn back if you're worried about making it home on your own. You can stay here and we will return to collect you when the mission has been successful. But if you do come with us, then that's it, you're with us to the end.'

Alexandra was silent for a moment, giving everyone in the group an opportunity to back out. Eleanor watched Stefan, thinking that he might volunteer to stay here, but he kept quiet. In a way, she wished he would stay here, so that she wouldn't feel guilty if anything did happen to him.

'Right,' resumed Alexandra. 'Everyone from the Greengrove Castle, I want you to forget your initial training on how to interact with others on social occasions. This is not the time for the kind of courtly behaviour we encouraged you to adopt when visiting another castle. The people in the wilderness can be extremely unpredictable. Never allow yourself to be thrown by their behaviour and make sure that you show no fear. Be polite, and open, but observe caution, too. Wherever possible follow Justin's lead . . . as he has experience of befriending these people.'

'It's not as frightening as you're making out,' said Justin. 'Most of them are perfectly friendly. The most important thing is not to scare them.'

✕

The group rode together to Handforth Grove. When they got there, they discovered two old women sitting on a large stone beneath a makeshift shelter. Justin approached them and said, 'Is there anyone in your community who knows about the White Castle?'

The first woman laughed. 'Poor Roger. This is his busiest day in years.'

Eleanor's heart sank. Justin asked, 'Someone else has spoken to him today?'

She nodded. 'Less than an hour ago. I can take you to him if you want. But only two of you. Roger's very old and he gets intimidated by large groups.'

He looked round. 'Eleanor, you come with me.'

Before anyone else had the chance to protest, he grabbed her hand and pulled her behind him. They followed the old woman as she led them behind the shelter into an incredibly complex shanty town. There was a mixture of the corrugated-iron shacks they had already seen during their travels, and smaller, more primitive constructions, little more than tents. Every tiny square of space was filled with adults, children or animals and the scent of tomato soup was so strong that Eleanor felt her stomach gurgle. The old woman moved fast, changing direction so rapidly that Eleanor worried she was deliberately trying to confuse them. Finally, she stopped outside a small blue shelter.

'Wait here,' she told them, and went inside. Moments

later she returned and said, 'Roger asks if you have any connection to the people who came here earlier.'

'I think so,' Justin replied. 'I don't know. Do you remember their names?'

'The two that came through to speak to Roger were a man named Basker and a woman named Sarah. Do you know them? Tell me the truth now, or he won't tell you anything.'

Justin sighed. 'Yes, we know them. Basker is my father and Sarah is Eleanor's friend.'

The woman went back into the shelter, then popped her head through the flap and told them to come inside. The shelter smelt so acrid that Eleanor wanted to pinch her nostrils but she worried if Roger saw her do this he would be insulted and refuse to tell them anything. So instead she tried not to breathe as Roger shuffled round on his mat and told them to sit down.

Eleanor couldn't tell how old Roger was. Although he had long white hair, his body and face were those of a younger man. He was wearing a pair of baggy orange trousers, but his chest and feet were bare and covered in blue tattoos.

'I've made a mistake, haven't I?' he said in a solemn voice.

Justin's nod was almost imperceptible.

'Damn,' he said. 'I knew it. It's my own fault. I knew this day would come, but I didn't realise there would be two groups. My dreams have let me down. I thought I simply had to decide whether or not to help your father. I didn't know I would have to choose between a father and a son. Is there anything I can do now?'

'It doesn't have to be too late,' said Justin. 'If you can think of a way of getting us there faster, before them, then maybe we could get even just a little bit of information.'

Roger was silent for a long time, before asking, 'What will your father do with what he finds in the White Castle?'

'I don't know.'

'OK,' he said. 'I cannot guarantee anything, but when I made the map for your father and his friend, I took the utmost care not to put them in any danger. The route I suggested was the safest, but also the slowest.'

'I have military training,' said Justin.

'Yes,' he said, 'you understand. I can offer no guarantees. You follow this other route at your own risk. Some of the terrain has never been covered before, as far as I know. There are two stretches, especially, one at the beginning, and one towards the end, that I do not know whether you will be able to cover, but if you can it should give you at least thirty minutes alone at the Castle before they arrive.'

'Thirty minutes?' said Eleanor. 'That's the best you can do?'

'They are almost an hour in front of you. I'm sorry. I wish I could do more.'

'Thirty minutes is fine,' said Justin. 'Thank you.'

'It will take me five minutes to prepare the map. I would prefer it if you returned to your friends and waited there.'

'Of course.'

They left the shelter and the old woman took them back through the shanty town to where they had left their friends. Eleanor explained what had happened and they waited for the woman to return with the map. When she did so, she said, 'Roger wants you to know that he hopes that you make it. He thinks that you will.'

'Say thank you to Roger for us,' said Justin. 'He has been extremely helpful, and he may just have changed the entire future of our country.'

The old woman nodded and left them to study the map.

CHAPTER EIGHTEEN

The map was very precise, telling them exactly how long it would take to travel each stretch and highlighting the dangers of each short cut. As he'd warned, the first stretch looked especially frightening, taking them across land that wasn't quite a swamp, but was clearly treacherous. There were warning signs saying the area was unstable and they saw what looked like potholes among the grass.

'What if it's toxic?' asked Eleanor. 'The guidebook warned that some vapours could cause death.'

'We have no choice,' said Justin. 'If you don't want to go.'

'No,' said Eleanor, 'I'm not afraid.'

'OK. We should go across in pairs. That way we won't strain the land too much.'

'I'll go first,' Eleanor told them, taking Stefan's hand. 'The two of us.'

'OK . . . the map says to avoid the holes.'

Eleanor laughed. 'That makes sense.'

'I'm not sure how solid it is,' said Justin, 'so tread extremely carefully.'

She squeezed Stefan's hand, not wanting him to be afraid. He smiled at her, and they stepped out onto the short cut. Eleanor was surprised that the ground wasn't marshy, but instead felt brittle, as if she was stepping on rotten wood. She held her breath, and the two of them took another step.

'How does it feel?' shouted Justin.

'Not good,' she said, 'I'm not sure we're all going to make it across.'

'Don't worry about that,' he said. 'Just keep going.'

They took another step. Stefan gripped Eleanor's hand even tighter. His palm was sweaty. She was relieved that there didn't appear to be any noxious vapours rising from this ground, and wondered why people were so scared of taking this short cut.

Then she heard Stefan scream.

CHAPTER NINETEEN

His scream was so loud that for a moment Eleanor didn't realise what was happening. Then the ground beneath her also gave way and she felt herself falling into a large pit. The sensation reminded her of falling into the oubliette at the Greengrove Castle, and the nightmares she'd had since that had happened. There was a horrible tension in her stomach, preparing herself for something terrible, but not knowing what. Time seemed to slow down and she wondered whether she would be falling for ever.

She landed well, feeling a shockwave go through her body as she hit the ground, but suffering no real pain. Stefan wasn't so lucky, and she heard an awful snapping sound followed by a terrible scream.

Eleanor turned towards him. He was sobbing and shaking and clutching his leg. She didn't know how to comfort him, so she wrapped her arms around his body. His trembling intensified. 'Stefan, listen to me,' she said.

'You've broken your leg. I realise you're in tremendous pain, but it will be OK. We will take care of you, I promise.' There was a beam of light coming from the hole above and as it hit Stefan's face Eleanor could see that he was drenched in sweat. His eyes were bulging and he was biting down into his lip. In a strange, babbling voice, he said, 'I love you, Eleanor.'

She hugged him back and without even thinking that there might be any intended romantic connotations to his words, she replied, 'I love you too, Stefan.'

Suddenly she heard Justin's voice screaming, 'Eleanor? Are you OK?'

'I'm fine,' she shouted back. 'But Stefan isn't.'

'How deep is it down there? Could I drop myself down?'

Eleanor's eyes adjusted to the darkness and she took in her surroundings. The floor was dry and she realised they were inside some sort of catacomb. There were lots of white bones and skulls packed into the curved brown walls, and as unpleasant as this situation was, she felt relieved that this was how her skeleton premonition had resolved itself.

Eleanor considered this. 'It's probably too deep for that.'

'But you managed it. To hell with it, I'm coming down.'

Justin's feet emerged through the hole. He was holding on to the earth above and as he released himself the drop no longer struck Eleanor as so deep. It was the surprise of falling that had made it so frightening. He landed well too, and came over to look at Stefan.

'I know,' Stefan said through sobs, 'I have to be left behind.'

'We'll get you back up,' he said, 'then take you to a physician. There has to be someone near here. Even people in the wilderness get sick.'

'I'm not sure we should move him,' said Eleanor.

'You're right. Someone should stay here with him while someone else goes to find a physician. We can afford that loss in numbers.' Justin seemed distracted, and said, 'What is this place?'

'A catacomb?' said Eleanor.

'Yeah, I know, but are there just dead bodies down here, or is it . . . ?'

'Is it what?'

He walked towards one of the brown walls. There was a large stone slab attached to the side. There were blue, white and red lines painted on the slab. 'What's this? It looks too elaborate to be a guide to the catacomb.' He tapped his fingernails against one of the lines. 'This image here, it's the Castle, isn't it?'

Eleanor couldn't see what he was pointing at. Justin studied the slab for a long while, then pulled out the map from his pocket and held it up alongside the lines. 'I don't believe it.'

'What?'

'Eleanor,' he said in an excited voice, 'you realise what you've discovered, don't you? This is a secret route right into the White Castle. If we use this we're bound to get there before my father does.'

'I didn't discover it,' she said. 'Stefan did.'

Justin looked at the boy on the floor. 'Yes, and he will get full recognition for this.'

Eleanor was concerned. 'But how do we know the route still works?'

'What do you mean?'

'Well, it's probably years since anyone's used it. There could be all kinds of obstructions.'

'You have a point. But I'm prepared to risk it.' He walked back across to the hole. 'Everyone, get down here. There's been a change of plan.'

'What about the horses?' asked Eleanor. 'Surely we won't be able to get them down here.'

'No,' said Justin, 'we'll tie them up and leave them here.'

'But what about the stuff at the Castle? Don't we need to load that onto the horses?'

'Look,' he told her, anger entering his voice, 'when we get to the Castle we can hide the stuff in the tunnel. Then bring it back slowly. It will be hard, and there will be stuff we won't be able to carry, but it'll be worth it for the extra time we'll gain. OK, Eleanor?'

She didn't like the tone he had adopted, but nodded anyway, seeing the sense in what he was suggesting. She turned back and said, 'This is all thanks to you, Stefan.'

Chapter Twenty

The adults dropped down into the tunnel first, helping the children follow them. Only Lucinda stayed above ground, heading off to find a physician for Stefan. Michael volunteered to stay with him, and the others assembled by the stone slab, waiting while Justin worked out how to follow the route.

'I'm sure there'll be more signs as we move on,' said Eleanor, anxious to get going.

'Yes, probably,' he replied, 'but I don't want to risk getting lost. Every second counts. Besides, I have it now. Come on.'

They ran down the tunnel. It was completely black inside and there was a terrible smell. Justin was ahead of everyone else and they all stopped when they heard him yelp in surprise and fall backwards.

'What is it?' asked Eleanor.

He didn't reply.

'Justin,' she said, in a worried voice, 'are you OK?'

'Yeah,' he said, 'it's not a proper wall, it feels weird. What is it?'

Zoran struck a match, and moved closer to the obstruction. Hephzi screamed.

'Shhh,' hissed Justin. 'Zoran, give me the matches.'

Although Eleanor was also scared by what she thought she saw, she forced herself to be brave and move forward with Justin. Another lit match illuminated what was blocking their path: a wall of dead crocodiles, green and yellow, piled up and packed tight so they filled the entire tunnel. Their skin and teeth were still intact, but their bloated bodies were coated with a thick slime. Eleanor saw some of the slime on Justin's face and felt sick.

Justin drew his sword. 'We have to hack our way through.'

'Oh,' said Hephzi, 'no, please, that's disgusting.'

'We have no choice. If you feel squeamish, stand back.'

Hephzi did so, putting her hands over her eyes. Eleanor took her sword and stood beside Justin. When he swung, she did too, and although the crocodiles were too tough to cut through completely, their actions revealed the wall's weaknesses and they focused their attention on these places. Justin turned his sword round and started hammering the hilt against a crocodile in the middle. It took several blows, but eventually it slipped backwards. Justin turned to Eleanor and said, 'I'm going to take a run at it.'

He walked back down the tunnel, stopped to take several deep breaths, then ran full pelt and body-slammed the wall of crocodiles. Another crocodile slid from the pile, but the wall still held. Justin was almost entirely coated in slime now and Eleanor was even more repulsed. He walked back to give it another try.

'Come on,' he urged, 'all of us. If we do it together, it's bound to fall.'

Eleanor walked back with the group, but deliberately stayed behind when they ran forwards, not wanting to end up covered in slime like Justin. More crocodiles slid downwards and Justin shouted, 'Again!'

Just as they were about to run forwards, Zoran turned to Alexandra (who seemed almost as repulsed as Eleanor by this whole business) and said, 'I don't think these crocodiles could've ended up in this position naturally. Someone's deliberately stacked them there as a barrier.'

'Even if Basker did discover this route,' she replied, 'he wouldn't have bothered to stop and do this.'

'I'm not talking about Basker,' said Zoran. 'What if people live in these tunnels?'

And as they ran forward, and the remainder of the crocodiles came tumbling down, Alexandra saw twenty-five pairs of eyes blinking at her and realised Zoran was right.

CHAPTER
TWENTY-ONE

The people in the tunnel didn't say anything. Eleanor thought she could see the glint of swords in their hands, and wondered if this was how they would meet their end, killed by a group of tunnel-dwelling scavengers. Around her, the group drew their swords. But Justin turned and gestured for everyone to put their weapons away. He took a deep breath and then shouted out, 'Don't be afraid. We're not here to attack you. We need your help.'

They waited for a moment, but there was no response. The tunnel people seemed to stay exactly where they were, and Eleanor got a strong sense they were waiting for something.

'Do you live here?' he tried.

Silence from the tunnel-people.

'That's OK, it's none of our business. We don't pose a threat to you.' He looked back at the group and then said, in a gentle, apologetic voice, 'We didn't mean to come into your home uninvited. We've only come down here because we want to get into the Castle.'

Eleanor suddenly realised that she could hear the people in the tunnel breathing. It sounded animalistic, inhuman. She wondered if they could understand the language Justin was speaking in.

'The Castle?' he repeated. 'We're following the directions . . . painted on the slab? We have a very good reason for needing to get inside it. If you could possibly help us, you would be doing a very good thing.'

They didn't seem to want to help. Justin sighed, exasperated. Eleanor tapped him on the shoulder. 'Maybe they don't speak English.'

He looked at her, and nodded. 'I think you might be right.' He handed her his sword and walked forward, knitting his hands behind his head. The tunnel-people shuffled backwards. He knelt down in the dirty water in front of them.

'See,' he said, 'it's safe.'

As he waited there, head bowed, four of the tunnel people walked closer towards them. Eleanor could see they were wrapped in dirty yellow and brown bandages, like mummies with exposed hands and faces. It was hard to make out their facial features, but one of them stopped and placed his hand on the back of Justin's head. Eleanor held her breath, waiting to see what would happen and hoping they wouldn't hurt him. The tunnel person withdrew his hand and, without warning, the tunnel people scattered, disappearing down dark passages to the left and right of Justin. He stood back up and returned to Eleanor. She could tell he was afraid.

'Could you see their faces?' she asked.

He shook his head. 'Not properly.'

'Were they human, do you think?'

He nodded. 'I'm certain of it. But I have a sense that they have been here for a very long time.'

'How did his hand feel, when he touched you?'

'Withered, but not horrible. It felt like he was trying to understand me.'

'What now?' asked Zoran.

Justin didn't respond for a long time, thinking his way around the problem. Eventually, he looked up and said in a confident voice, 'My feeling is that we have to go forward. We're only afraid because we're confronting the unknown. But I think we have to assume that they mean us no harm. I gave them a chance to attack me and they didn't take it. So I think we're safe.'

Hedley came forward and said, in a slightly sceptical voice, 'You're right. That's the only thing we can do if we want to get to the Castle before Basker. But I pray you're right about these people being friendly. For all our sakes.'

CHAPTER TWENTY-TWO

They continued their journey, entering a different tunnel that was illuminated by candles placed in small holes along the wall.

'Where do you think they got the candles from?' Eleanor asked Justin.

'Probably from inside the Castle.'

'You think the tunnel people go into the Castle then?'

Justin nodded. 'It would make sense. If they're the ones who put up the slabs with directions and the slabs haven't already been there for hundreds of years.'

Eleanor sensed that he didn't really want to waste time talking to her. She knew he was psyching himself up for the next surprise, but the way she was coping with her own fear was by acting normal and pretending this situation was nothing unusual. She felt slightly hurt by the way Justin was acting with her, and walked back to James, who was lurking at the rear of the group. He looked exhausted, and she remembered the time at the

Kingmaker's Castle when he told her how happy he was that his life consisted of nothing more strenuous than sitting in his tower and reading books. She felt sorry for him and regretted recruiting him for this mission. Wanting to comfort him, Eleanor touched his arm. He flinched.

'Oh,' she said, 'I'm sorry, I didn't mean to startle you.'

He shrugged. 'You didn't really. I'm just a bit on edge.'

'I don't blame you. This is the scariest thing that's happened since . . . well, ever.'

Eleanor was pleased to hear James laugh at this and, emboldened, asked him, 'Who do you think makes a better leader, Alexandra or Hedley?'

He seemed amused by this question and said, 'I'm surprised Hedley let her take over. It's very out of character for her.'

'Hey, James, guess what? I've just had a really great idea.'

'What's that, Eleanor?'

'Why don't your four join our group all the time? Then we'd be the Castle Eight. It would be brilliant. You could come on all our expeditions. They're not all like this, honest. Well, to tell the truth, the only time everything's gone completely to plan was when we visited you, but it would be different if you were part of the group.'

'Eleanor,' he said, raising his hand, 'two things, OK?'

'Yes?'

'First, let's get to the end of this adventure before planning another one.'

'And the second thing?'

He put on a mock-angry voice. 'There's no way I'm ever coming anywhere with you ever again. In fact, I'm not even going to leave my tower.'

Eleanor felt pleased she'd had this conversation with James and remained alongside him until they came across their second obstacle. Once again, a haphazardly erected wall blocked their passage, only this time it wasn't made out of crocodiles but instead of small boxes that were so different from anything Eleanor had ever seen before that she wondered whether they had come from space. James immediately left Eleanor's side and ran towards them.

'Oh,' he said, 'I can't believe it. I knew some of these must exist somewhere, but I never thought I'd actually see one.'

'What are they?' asked Jonathan.

'Computers,' he said, and when no one responded, he turned and told them, 'boxes of information. Storage systems. Inside each one of these machines there could be untold riches.'

Zoran withdrew his sword. 'Step back.'

James took a moment to realise what he was doing, and then stopped him. 'No, Zoran, I don't mean literally "inside" . . . well, I do, I suppose, but you're not going to get to it by cutting them open.'

'Then how do we get the riches?"

'Electricity. We need to go somewhere with electricity. We have ways of generating electricity at the Kingmaker's Castle, but it's very primitive, and we might not be able to make enough to power these systems. Still, the important thing is to preserve these machines.'

'James, don't get distracted,' Justin told him. 'This is nothing compared to what we might discover inside the Castle.'

'How do you know? This could be the most important thing in there.'

'Maybe, or they could be broken beyond all repair. Who knows how long they've been here?'

James shook his head. 'I don't think it matters. I'm certain there's a way of retrieving the information from these machines. We have manuals in our library, from a different time. The language is hard to understand, but maybe over years . . .'

'It could take hundreds of years, James,' Justin replied, 'and in the meantime we could be missing out on stuff that could be far more immediately accessible.'

'What are you suggesting? That we leave these computers here?"

'No, I'm happy for you to stay here . . . with someone else . . . and shift as many of these machines back to where Stefan's waiting with Lucinda. But maybe the tunnel people won't take kindly to you stealing their property.'

This had the desired effect. James clearly had no desire to face the tunnel people alone, and he reluctantly agreed to leave the computers behind. Justin kicked the wall of machines as hard as he could, and they tumbled to the floor.

CHAPTER
TWENTY-THREE

Behind this second wall wasn't
another group of tunnel dwellers, but a single woman.
Instead of skulking in the darkness she stood illuminated,
just beyond where the computers had fallen. She was older
than Alexandra and Hedley, but not, Eleanor realised, an
old woman. Her hair and skin were extremely fair, the hair
not quite white, but neither blonde. Her blue eyes and red
lips provided her face with the only colour. From a distance, her scarlet clothes looked like rags, not that dissimi-
lar from the bandages the tunnel people had sported, but
as Eleanor examined them more closely, she realised they
had been stitched together from many layers, the pattern-
ing beautifully intricate. As she stared at the woman's face,
she thought she recognised something about her.

The woman spoke. 'My people said you needed my
help.'

Justin walked forward. 'Yes, that's true. We need to
get inside the Castle.'

'You are not the first.'

'We know. The others . . . the ones that came today . . . they are bad people.'

'Others came today?' she asked, her voice betraying surprise. 'I didn't know that. They didn't come this way.'

'No,' said Justin, 'they are above ground. They are on their way now.'

'It is possible to enter the Castle above ground,' she said. 'Difficult. But it is only access that is the problem. If they are athletic . . . There is no protection there. They do not need it. People are afraid.'

'Yes,' said Sophie suddenly. 'It is the same where we are from. Our castle.'

Eleanor noticed the way Sophie was emulating the tunnel woman's clipped speech and smiled to herself. It amused her to see them behaving in this way. Mary caught her eye and returned the smile. She wondered if Mary was amused by the same thing and assumed she probably was. This made her feel close to her friend again. Although Eleanor had once had untold admiration for the Kingmaker's Quartet, she idolised them less now, seeing them, like the people from her own castle, as fallible human beings. It occurred to her that she shouldn't be having such idle thoughts at a time like this, but couldn't help it: the tension was making her mind misbehave.

'Which castle are you from?'

'Kingmaker's,' said Sophie.

'Ah, Kingmaker's,' the woman repeated in a dreamy voice. 'You are descendants of the original inhabitants, right? Remaining in your castle while the country changes around you? Oblivious to the turmoil, and safe because of some scary story your foresighted forefathers spread as they knew this day would come?'

Sophie interrupted her reverie. 'No. The Castle was abandoned when we came to it. Well, when James and Stewart did . . . we moved there later. It had been empty for hundreds of years.'

'Hundreds?' said the woman, sounding shocked. 'That doesn't make sense.'

'We can't be specific,' James admitted. 'The records we have . . . it's an inexact science.'

'Now I really don't understand,' said the woman. 'Tell me this, are you all from the Kingmaker's Castle?'

'No,' said Jonathan. 'Some of us are from the Clearheart Castle.'

'Clearheart?' she said, even more astonished. 'What are you doing here? And what possible connection could you have with the Kingmaker's Castle.'

'We are friends,' said Eleanor.

The woman shook her head. 'The country has changed many times while we've been here. Do any of you know anyone from before the fall of the kingdom?'

Eleanor felt James place his hand on her shoulder and realised they were going to lie.

'No,' said James, 'we don't.'

'Then how do you even know about this castle? Are there records in Kingmaker's?'

'No,' said Justin. 'I discovered its existence through my travelling . . . my explorations.'

'Your explorations,' she repeated, as if testing the word. 'And you're from Clearheart too?'

'No.' He smiled. 'Greengrove.'

This did not meet with a warm response. Although it was physically impossible for the woman to turn any paler, she looked sickened and asked, 'What is your surname?'

He looked awkward. 'Basker.'

'No,' she said, 'I don't believe it. The line died out. After everything your ancestors did . . . the punishment was just.'

Justin responded quickly. 'You know my name?'

'Yes.'

'Then I need you to understand that I bear it like a curse. And the person you need to stop getting into the Castle is my father. He's the one who's above ground. We have to get inside before him. It's the only way to save the Castle, and the secrets inside it.'

The woman came forward and placed her hand on his forehead. Moments later, seemingly satisfied, she said, 'You are telling the truth. You are different. The first honest man from your family line. Come with me. I will show you how to enter the Castle.'

CHAPTER
TWENTY-FOUR

The woman ran ahead, dragging Justin by the hand. Eleanor was just behind them, with the rest of the group struggling to keep up. Justin and the woman were talking to each other at great speed, but no matter how hard she tried Eleanor couldn't hear what they were saying.

Soon the tunnel changed and instead of seeming as if it had been carved out of the earth, it suddenly had white tiled walls, covered in a dense layer of mould. Eleanor saw a sign obscured by dirt: the only letters visible were T W LL. She could see daylight through the opening ahead and they all ran faster.

Then Justin stopped and he heard her say to the woman, 'I thought this tunnel would take us all the way into the Castle.'

'No, no,' she said, 'you still have to go round to the entrances. There's more than one of them, it's complicated . . .'

He looked round. 'Are we ahead of the other group?'

'I don't know. There's only one way to find out.'

They went through the opening and Eleanor saw a row of twisted metal railings and behind that a large patch of overgrown grass, obscuring a stone wall which had several arrow-loops. She didn't have time to take in her surroundings as Justin urged her to climb up some broken wooden steps that led up to a walkway. The rotten wood was hard to walk across, and Eleanor feared it would give way beneath her at any minute.

'When we get inside the grounds,' Justin told the group, 'there are several towers and no doubt items of great interest in every single one, but I want us all to concentrate on getting into the White Castle. According to the stories, that's where all the important stuff is stored, and that's what we need.'

'Are the Crown Jewels there?' Zoran asked, scratching his stubble.

The woman stared at Zoran, clearly amazed. 'You're not going to take things from the Castle?'

'That's why we're here,' he said. 'If we don't take it, my father will.'

Eleanor thought Justin was being too brusque with the woman and felt relieved when James stepped forward and said, 'Now that everyone knows there are valuable objects inside the Castle they are no longer safe. We don't intend to steal them, but to remove them from here and take them to the Kingmaker's Castle as a temporary measure . . . until it is safe for them to be returned.'

The woman seemed pacified by this and said, 'We have been here so long, uninterrupted by almost anyone, that I forgot that this day must come. The rest of the country has fallen . . . why should here be any different?'

As she said this, a giant raven hopped up onto the stairs behind Justin. The bird's feathers and beak were ink black.

'The story was true, if you're interested,' the woman told the group. 'They left just before the fall of the kingdom, as was always predicted. Twenty years ago, they came back. I remember the exact day. Everyone was astonished, especially those among my people who knew why they had gone in the first place. We saw it as a good omen and waited for some sort of saviour, but then no one came and we realised it wasn't a sign of anything at all . . . just something strange that happened.

'You should know there was a time, long ago, between the ages, when this building was a different sort of repository . . . one that was open to all. A former era of democracy. There are those who believe . . . how does it go . . . that the reason why everything ended was because we failed to heed the dangers of dissemination, and it was the conception of this dissemination that led to the ultimate catastrophe. The wine argument . . . do you know it?'

Everyone looked at Zoran. He shook his head.

'A bottle of wine,' she said. 'It's enough for three or four people.'

'One, in his case,' muttered Jonathan to Eleanor, pointing at Zoran.

'But if we want this wine to be shared by a thousand people, we have to put water in it, and then it becomes useless. Some people believe the same is true of information.'

'My father believes that,' said Justin, 'but I do not.'

'I realise that,' she said. 'But you must be careful. If the people find out too much too quickly, it could cause chaos. You have to know how to get these ideas to the people.'

'We will be careful,' said James. 'It is a question we shall ponder at great length before taking any action.'

'But now we must continue,' Justin urged them. 'We must head to the White Castle.'

The woman stepped back. 'I am sorry, but I must leave you here. I cannot travel any further with you . . . my people would never forgive me. But I shall tell them that your motives are pure and I give you my guarantee that they will not harm you as you make your way back. I hope you find everything you are looking for. You would not be the first to come to the White Castle looking for an answer and end up going away with disappointment in your hearts.'

'Thank you for bringing us here,' said Justin. 'You will not be disappointed in us.'

The woman nodded, and walked away.

CHAPTER TWENTY-FIVE

When they entered the Castle's grounds, Eleanor was amazed to see the remains of what looked like a small village, clearly more elaborate in its original construction than anything she'd seen before. As Justin had warned them, there were many towers around the sides of the square, but it was clear where they had to go to get inside: the White Castle, at the centre. Although it was in serious disrepair, Eleanor could see three elaborate weathervanes at the top, just about remaining upright, and a tattered flag.

'Quick,' shouted Justin, 'get inside. We must do it now. Look, Basker and his army are here.'

Eleanor turned and saw soldiers surrounding each of the many other towers. She didn't understand why they weren't heading straight to the White Castle and worried Justin had got things wrong.

'Are you certain all the important stuff is in the White Castle?' she asked him.

'Yes. Go there. Now!'

Eleanor did as he instructed, running across the overgrown grass to the Castle. There was another rotten staircase that looked even harder to climb than the one that had brought them into the grounds. She jumped up past the first two broken steps and landed safely on the third.

'Go up one at a time,' Justin shouted to the group. 'It won't hold for any more than that.'

Eleanor made her way up the steps. When she reached the entrance she ran inside, and uncertain what to do next, waited for Justin to come up behind her. The first room was filled with cannons and guns.

'Should we take these things?' she asked. 'The weapons?'

'No,' he said, 'keep going up. There's a stairwell in the corner.'

Eleanor ran across and went up the stone steps. When she reached the top she saw something so terrifying that she screamed out loud.

'What's wrong, Eleanor?' Justin asked, running up behind her.

She pointed at the cabinet. Behind a thin layer of glass there were twenty severed heads. Each face was bearded and sinister, with haircuts that clearly came from a different age. The sight was so horrible that Eleanor's knees felt weak. She turned round and was amazed to see Justin laughing. Before she had chance to ask him what was so funny he banged the hilt of his sword against the glass with incredible force. It shattered, and he reached in to pick up a head.

'Justin,' she scowled, 'don't!'

He ignored her protests and turned and threw the head at her. 'It's plastic,' he said, 'or maybe wood. Either way, it's not real. Don't be afraid.'

Eleanor felt silly, and cross with Justin for his lack of sympathy. She continued round the corner and found a stable filled with plastic or wooden horses. There were ten of them, each with a red banner above emblazoned with a name in gold lettering. The first horse was brown and had the name William I above it; the second black with Edward I; the third yellow, Edward V; the fourth brown, Henry VII; the fifth black, Henry VIII; the sixth grey, Edward VI; the seventh brown, James I; the eighth yellow, Charles I; the ninth brown, Charles II, the tenth black, William III. Eleanor stood staring at the horses, looking for a clue as to what the names meant. Former kings? That seemed the only possibility. Under the last name was the date 1689 to 1702. Eleanor realised this was an old Anno Domini date, and remembered that the guidebook she had been reading at the Kingmaker's Castle had been written in 1885 – so did this mean that the kingdom had fallen in 1702, and it had taken one hundred and eighty-three years for London to have disintegrated?

Justin urged her on.

'Upstairs, Eleanor. This stuff isn't important either.'

She ran up to the next level, and found it empty. She turned to Justin and said, 'There's nothing here.'

'I can see that. Go up again.'

She did so. The next floor was nearly empty too. All that remained were a long, spiked mace and two suits of armour. Justin stamped on the floor. 'Damn it! They must have got here before us. I can't believe it. How could they have had the time to get all the stuff out?'

'Maybe it isn't here,' she said. 'Maybe it's been moved into those towers.'

'No,' he said, 'that doesn't make sense. All the stories said that everything we needed was stored in the White Castle.'

'What if someone else knew they were coming? That woman who helped us. She could've been in league with your father. She might have deliberately led us into this Castle as a trap.'

'I didn't want to say anything to her,' said Eleanor, 'but I'm fairly certain that tunnel woman must have been related to them.'

'Who?'

'The last royal family . . . before the fall of the kingdom . . . which means she's related to Sarah . . . so if

Basker and Sarah had approached her, then it would be perfectly possible that she'd take Sarah's side and want to trick us.'

The rest of the group came up behind them. Jonathan ran to a window. 'Look,' he said, pointing downwards.

They all crowded round the window. At first, Eleanor thought he wanted her to look at all the soldiers emerging from the various towers, holding their treasures high above their heads like a stream of successful worker ants. The hoard they were taking looked just as exciting as they had been led to believe, and her heart hurt as she saw all the paintings and ten times more books than the Kingmaker's Quartet had in their library, and computers and filing cabinets and other machines with screens, and diamonds and crowns and weapons and caskets filled with gold. She realised these last items were the Crown Jewels, and they were incredibly impressive, although she was more upset about the failure of the mission than the loss of the treasure, no matter how beautiful it looked and how much she would have loved to have worn one of the crowns, even if only for a moment. But this wasn't what her father wanted her to witness. So she dragged her eyes away from the booty and looked again, and saw what frightened him: a different group of soldiers approaching the White Castle with flaming torches.

'They're going to set it alight,' shouted Jonathan.

'No,' said Justin, 'they can't. There's barrels of gunpowder here. If they set the Castle alight we'll all die!'

He threw the window open. Eleanor noticed his father standing on the grass below.

'Dad!' he screamed. 'Don't do it. We're in here. If you burn the Castle down, you'll kill us.'

Basker smiled, and in a jovial voice that chilled Eleanor, he said, 'That's the idea, son.'

Chapter
Twenty-Six

When Sarah had abandoned
the Castle Five, she had done so for what she considered
noble reasons. She knew she was betraying her friends,
but she had convinced herself that she was doing this for
the good of her country. Of course, there were also personal reasons for the shift of allegiances, but she was
optimistic that everything would be happily resolved.
Sarah's mother, Hildegard, brought her to the Greengrove Community at an early age. She had died soon
after, and they'd never had an opportunity to discuss her
decision, but Sarah's childhood memories of the Daughters' Community were of a stiff, sad place, where her
every move was scrutinised and where it was impossible
to do anything without being forced to consider the
weight of history. In contrast, her life at the Greengrove
Community had been happy and free and while she'd
never been allowed to forget that she was special it
wasn't a burden in the same way. Then, when she was

sixteen, she met Anderson. She had never talked to Alexandra about her romance with Anderson, and she doubted that Alexandra even knew it had happened. Anderson had talked about Alexandra a lot, how she was his childhood sweetheart, how she'd broken his heart, how Sarah was the first person who'd convinced him that he might love again. He was older than Sarah, and while she was flattered by his attentions, she couldn't help finding him impossibly serious. Sarah was serious too, but she resented the psychological presence in their relationship of this woman she had never met. Eventually she grew tired of the comparisons, and they stopped going out. When, a few years later, she met Alexandra, she was amazed that this funny, good-natured, down-to-earth woman had caused Anderson so much inner turmoil, especially given the age difference, and assumed it must have come from childhood confusion rather than deliberate malice. She often wondered if Anderson had also had a romantic relationship with Lucinda, but he had never mentioned anything. She had only recently come to the Clearheart Community when she joined the Castle Seven, but it was always possible that he had gone to the inn she had worked in on his travels, and now she thought about it, she remembered the innkeeper saying something to Anderson about how he had been in there before, although he did not say if that had happened while Lucinda had been working there.

Anderson, like Sarah, was being watched over by a small group of elders in their community. They were the closest thing the Clearheart Community had to rulers, the people who gave orders to the small army and stopped the community dissolving into anarchy. There was little crime in their community – no murders, few robberies, just the odd dispute usually brought about by drink. The problem for these rulers was that like most communities they had to decide what to do about the outside world. The Greengrove Community had had many years of peace, but most people seemed to believe that this couldn't last for ever. The fall of the kingdom had traumatised England, and for a very, very long time all anyone had been interested in was survival and rebuilding. But the elders had an instinctive sense that this period was coming to an end, and so they met with Anderson and asked him to form a special group, the Castle Seven. Sarah had been happy to join, and as long as Anderson was the unofficial leader of the group, she had felt secure following his instructions. But after he had betrayed them, the Castle Six had seemed to fall apart. Although Alexandra had accused her of being a snob and she'd been forced to back down, she knew the problem had started when they agreed to let Eleanor's father join the group. Eleanor was an extraordinary person, but Sarah couldn't believe that she had inherited her skills from her parents, who seemed such awful people. And as the rest of the group continued to ignore her sensible advice, the allure of returning to the Daughters' Castle had become increasingly strong. For years, she had torn up the invitations that had arrived for their anniversary parties, but now she wondered whether she would receive greater appreciation from her own kind. And now she had this information about the White Castle, she thought it was the best time to return. They would accept her, celebrate her and love her. And if it was the Daughters' Community that changed the country's future instead of the Clearheart Community, what real difference did it make? As long as she was part of it.

The one thing that Sarah had put out of her mind as she rode to the Daughters' Castle was their alleged allegiance with Basker. It was hard for her to see him as anything but a villain, especially after the way he had trapped them when they visited their castle. She knew he saw himself as some sort of aristocratic politician, but that was laughable. His behaviour was shabby, and she couldn't believe the Daughters would have anything to do with him. Sophie at the Kingmaker's Castle had claimed her source there had said there was a link, but she could easily have been lying, and if not, the quartet there were almost as incompetent as the Castle Five and she could easily be mistaken. Sarah knew that she had to go by her instinct, and her instinct told her she was doing the right thing.

✕

As she drew closer to the Daughters' Castle, Sarah became aware that she was being followed. Two dark-haired women on black horses were riding behind her, and going so fast that they soon overtook her and forced her to stop.

'It's OK,' she said, 'I'm one of you.'

The first woman pushed a long, thick plait over her shoulder and, raising an eyebrow, asked, 'One of whom?'

'My name is Sarah,' she explained. 'I'm the great-great granddaughter of the last princess before the fall of the kingdom. I used to live here . . . with my mother. Her name was Hildegard.'

Neither woman seemed to recognise the name. The first woman turned to her friend, and they rode slightly away from her. They talked for a short while, and then the second woman rode off. The first woman returned and said to Sarah, 'Wait here with me. It won't take long, and if you are who you say you are, there will be no trouble.'

Sarah sighed, and they remained there, not talking until the second woman returned with three white-haired older women, all riding black horses. One of these women looked familiar, and said in a bright voice, 'Sarah! You've come back to us. Do you remember me? My name is Stephanie. I looked after you when you were a little girl.'

With these words, several years' worth of memories suddenly returned, and feeling tearful Sarah embraced Stephanie and said, 'Is there somewhere we can go to talk? I have something really important to tell all of you.'

Maybe, Sarah realised now, she should have been more careful. The excitement of being accepted stopped her from exercising her usual caution and it didn't even occur to her to check with them about whether they had any connection with Basker before telling them what she had discovered.

And when she saw him at their head table when they went for their evening meal, she had still tried to pretend it didn't mean anything. Basker didn't recognise her at first, even though at the Greengrove Castle he had spent two long days arguing with the Castle Seven about how they would divide up England between them, and had sat opposite Sarah for a long period of that meeting.

When he did realise who she was, Basker smiled, and then later in the evening, after dessert and coffee, getting her alone, he came across for a conversation. To her surprise, he started by apologising for the 'unpleasant business' at the Greengrove Castle, claiming he had changed a lot since then.

She could see how he had charmed the Daughters, and knew immediately that it would be dangerous to tell them how she truly felt about this man. Instead she responded politely and made some jokes about the general fecklessness of the Castle Five.

At the end of the evening, she retired to her room and wondered how she could salvage this situation. The Daughters were planning to leave the following morning, no doubt accompanied by Basker and his army. The Clearheart Castle party had a day on them: there was always the possibility that they might get to the White Castle first. But in her heart she knew this wouldn't happen. The Daughters were much more efficient. The Clearheart group could have a two-day lead and it still wouldn't make any difference.

When they set out on their expedition to the White Castle, there was no discussion about what would happen if or, as was more likely, when they ran into the other group of travellers. And Sarah's concern for her friends diminished even further after the excitement of being introduced to the pale, nearly white-haired woman in scarlet clothes who lived in her tunnels. This woman, it seemed, was her aunt, whom she had never met.

'I had no idea,' said Sarah, as she was introduced to her. 'I didn't even know my mother had a sister.'

The woman laughed. 'That doesn't surprise me. Hildegard was never that interested in her family.'

Sarah ignored the direct criticism of her mother, and explained, 'Yes, but she never told me that there was this other possibility.'

'What possibility, dear?'

'That instead of living at the Clearheart Castle, or with the Daughters, I could come with you and stay here.'

'Would you really have wanted to live in a tunnel?' she asked.

Sarah smiled. 'Well, no, but you do have the Castle too. Even if you're too scared to live in it, you must sleep in it sometimes?'

The woman nodded. 'Yes, that's true.'

To Sarah's credit, she had no idea of the depth of hatred Basker now felt towards his son, and until she saw the soldiers – walking, it somehow seemed, in agonising slow motion – going across to ignite the White Castle, she fooled herself that he wouldn't want to harm anyone from the Clearheart Community. Surely the fact that he had tricked them, sending six soldiers ahead of the slower-moving main party to clear the contents of the Castle into the surrounding towers ready for them to pick everything up and transport it to the Daughters' Castle would be victory enough? But no, it seemed not. And, as he had immediately instructed a soldier to hold a sword across Sarah's throat when she discovered the full extent of his evil lest she try to help, there really was nothing she could do about it.

Chapter Twenty-Seven

After he had informed Eleanor and Justin that he wanted them to die in the White Castle, Basker led his army and followers away. As terrified as Eleanor was, she remained clear-minded enough to wonder whether this was because he was squeamish, certain of his victory, or simply eager that no one should turn against him after witnessing the horror of his enemies being burned alive. She also entertained the thought that maybe he actually hoped they would escape: that this might still, after all, be merely a bizarre test he was inflicting on his son. Her reason for wondering this was that Basker was being surprisingly sloppy for a supposedly murderous man. If he hadn't left the suits of armour and spiked mace in the Castle deliberately, if they were merely a few objects dropped or abandoned during the ransacking, then it seemed an odd oversight. Eleanor immediately grabbed the cuirass of one suit and said, 'If two of us put these on, we can go downstairs and try to put the fire out.'

'No,' said Justin, 'that's not a good idea. As soon as that gunpowder explodes, it won't matter what you're wearing.'

As soon as he said that Eleanor's calm disappeared and she woke up to the realisation that she was trapped inside a burning castle. In a panicked voice she shouted, 'Well, what are we going to do?'

'Please calm down, Eleanor,' he told her. 'I'm thinking.'

Eleanor noticed her father was staring through a window on the other side of the building. 'What is it, Dad?' she asked. 'Do you have an idea?'

'Yeah,' he replied, 'that tree. If we could get across to it, it should be easy to climb down.'

Eleanor and Justin went across to the window. There was a huge, thick white tree with a large curve in its trunk growing close to the Castle.

'Yes,' he told Jonathan, after appraising the situation, 'I think you might be right.'

'So how do we get there?' asked Eleanor.

Justin didn't reply. Instead, he walked across to the spiked mace, picked it up and went over to where Jonathan was standing. He checked the distance, then, using all his force, smashed the mace through the window. He then aimed it at the trunk, and buried it into the bark so that one end of the mace was wedged against the stone ledge and the other held fast by the tree.

'Is this going to work?' Alexandra asked.

'It's our only option,' said Jonathan, 'unless you want to risk running through the flames.'

'You should be OK,' said Justin. 'Just don't look down.'

He stood up on the ledge. He smashed the rest of the glass in the window and grabbed hold of the mace, dangling from it for a moment before throwing himself into the tree. It twanged as he made it across, but to everyone's relief, it didn't fall or break.

'He did it,' said Hephzi, stepping up onto the window ledge. 'And if he managed it, we can too.'

One by one, the group swung from the Castle to the tree, and then made their way down to the ground. Eleanor waited until last, and ignored Justin's advice, looking down before she grabbed hold of the mace. She had a horrible moment of vertigo as she calculated the distance to the ground and her stomach lurched as she moved across, but she reached the tree safely, and shimmied down the bark with ease.

Chapter Twenty-Eight

Lucinda had had surprisingly little difficulty in finding a physician. The first few people she asked didn't understand her request, but then someone realised what she meant, grabbed hold of her hand and pulled her back round the shanty town until they were outside the home of a man who – her guide insisted – was a 'doctor'.

He was a young man, wearing blue trousers with a brown leather belt that had an elaborate silver buckle. His white shirt was immaculately clean, in contrast to the dirty outfits of most of the people who lived in the shanty town. When he saw Lucinda, he came forward and put his hands on her waist. This over-familiarity shocked her slightly and she was relieved when he asked, 'How can I help you?'

She pulled away. 'It's my friend . . . he had an accident . . . he fell through the ground . . . I think he broke his leg.'

'OK,' he said, 'don't panic. Where did it happen? Is he far from here?'

'No,' she said, 'not too far. I'll show you.'

The physician grabbed a leather bag from his shack and the two of them left together. 'We need to get a couple of people to help us. Don't worry, it won't take long. Is someone with him?'

Lucinda nodded.

When they reached the hole, Michael shouted up that he was worried about Stefan because he had passed out.

'Don't worry,' the physician said. 'That's a natural reaction. And it'll make it easier for us to move him.'

'Poor Stefan,' remarked Lucinda. 'He's always the one that bad things happen to.'

The physician nodded. 'Well, often that's the way it works. Have you ever studied the System?'

'No,' she said, 'but a friend of mine called Sophie is an expert on it. She says that it was one of the silly things people used to believe but they don't any more.'

The doctor's expression changed, and Lucinda worried she had insulted him. 'Well, yes, you would be silly to follow it slavishly, but I think any source of information or wisdom that people have spent hundreds of years formulating has something to offer.'

Lucinda tried to look contrite. 'I'm sure you're right.'

He nodded. 'Now, let's take a look at this boy.'

CHAPTER TWENTY-NINE

Everyone was watching Justin. This had become his mission, and it was obvious that he was the one who would feel their failure most keenly. Not only did he have the loss to deal with, but he also had to come to terms with the fact that if his father had intended to kill him, it was likely that once he discovered that he was still alive, he would try again. Clearly wanting to get away from the others, Justin jumped up onto his horse and told Eleanor to ride with him for a moment.

'Are you OK, Justin?' she asked.

'Yes,' he replied. 'I'm fine, and don't worry, I have a plan. We can't leave here yet in case some of the soldiers are still here and one of them sees us . . . but this doesn't have to be a disaster. The way I see it, there are two possible responses we could make to what has happened. The first is to find some way of getting the stuff my father took from the White Castle back from him.'

'Justin,' said Eleanor gently.

He ignored her. 'Obviously, that's going to be diffi-cult, we'd have to recruit an army from somewhere if we were going to stand a chance. There's no point attacking him on the way back, but maybe later we could invade the Daughters' Castle . . . I assume that's where they're going to be storing it.'

'Please . . .' she said.

'Or the second response,' he continued, 'is . . . well, there's something else I didn't tell you when I came to your community. You know I said I had been travelling really widely in England, and that's how I found out about the White Castle?'

Eleanor nodded.

'Well, I discovered something else too. There's a group of people, from one of the wilderness areas, who produce boats. You know what a boat is, don't you?'

'Yes, Justin, I know what a boat is.'

'OK. Well, if you give them enough money . . . I'm not sure what currency they use, but I can find out . . . actually, it's more likely to be a barter system, but still . . . the point is, if you pay them, they'll produce a boat for you. And although no one's come back yet so we don't know if anyone's been successful, in theory, it should be possible to get to another country.'

'Justin . . .'

'All the atlases I've looked at are from a long time ago, so I don't know what it's like in other kingdoms . . . we

talked about this before, remember, when we first met?'
He looked at Eleanor. She nodded. 'But what I'm saying
is . . . the fall of the kingdom, it was only this kingdom.
Who knows what's out there, Eleanor? Probably much
more important things about our history and culture
than anything my father has discovered. We might even
find someone who could invade England, but like a
benign invasion, and they could overthrow my father
and . . .'

'Justin, what exactly are you asking me to do?'

'I'm asking you to come with me, to get in a boat,
leave England, and sail to another country.'

He looked at her with hope in his eyes.

'I'm sorry,' she said softly. 'I can't do that.'

'Why not?'

'Remember when I came to the Greengrove Castle
and I asked you to leave your family and come back
with me and you said you couldn't do it because in spite
of everything Basker had done to you, you still couldn't
leave your family?'

He shook his head dismissively. 'Yes, but Eleanor,
that's got nothing to do with this.'

'It has, Justin. I have a responsibility to my family, my
community, the Castle Five . . . or Four, as they now are.
When we go back home, it's going to be difficult. This
mission was supposed to redeem us in the eyes of everyone who lives in our community, and instead it's proved

a disaster. I know you hate facing up to failure . . . and that's a good quality, but . . .'

'That's not what this is about, Eleanor. I know you think I'm just haring off on another mission because this one didn't work and I can never go home again, but it's not true . . . I really believe this is the only way I can save our country.'

'And I believe in you, Justin. But you're going to have to do this alone.'

Justin bit a fingernail. 'I didn't want to have to say this, Eleanor, but you've left me no choice. If you don't come with me, this is going to be the end of our relationship.'

'Oh, Justin,' she said, 'don't be like that.'

'I'm sorry, Eleanor, I . . .' His voice grew angry again. 'That's the way it is, OK? I don't know how long I'm going to be gone, and if you're not prepared to follow me, then . . .'

'Justin, you're being childish. I love you. Doesn't that count for anything?'

He ignored her question, turned round, and got up on his horse. She shouted out to him about how he said they had to wait if they didn't want to be noticed by Basker's soldiers but he remained silent. It wasn't until he had disappeared from view that she realised he hadn't even given her a goodbye kiss.

CHAPTER THIRTY

They waited there for an hour, then went back to try to find Stefan and Lucinda. The physician had made Stefan a splint, bandaged his leg, and lifted him from the hole. He would be able to ride on the back of someone else's horse, as long as they went slowly. There was no hurry now anyway, and the only place they had to get to was the nearest inn.

When they arrived at an inn, Jonathan asked everyone to meet in the bar for a conversation. No one was eager to do this. Everyone was tired, and deflated, and the Kingmaker's Quartet were already mumbling about leaving the group and going home. James was keen to return to the tunnel and pick up the computers, but this suggestion was ignored.

Jonathan asked the barmaid to fetch everyone drinks, then stood up and addressed the group. 'I realise how serious this seems. But I want everyone to know that this mission was not as important as we made it out to be. Now Justin has gone it's easy for me to see that he agitated us into seeing this quest as a make-or-break mission. But the truth is, this isn't even something that we really should've been involved with . . . obviously I'm addressing the Clearheart Community here more than the people from Kingmaker's. As I understand it, the Castle Seven was originally set up as a way of maintaining friendly relationships between communities. We are a relatively small castle, and it shouldn't be up to us to be the peacekeepers for the whole of England. Sure, no one wants Basker to succeed in controlling the country, but he still has a long way to go before he achieves that aim. When we return to our community, we should be proud about what we've done. This is how we'll face the dissenters . . . by pointing out how small our role should be, and how we're doing something that they don't want to do on their behalf.'

Eleanor looked round the group. It was obvious her father's words weren't getting through, and that he'd missed something important. Something that Zoran had to raise. 'You're forgetting what we told the Community. They expect us to come back with untold riches . . . the Crown Jewels!'

'Yes, I know, Zoran. And we'll just have to deal with people's expectations. It's not as if we discovered there weren't any jewels. As far as we know, Basker's got them, and everyone in the Community knows how evil he is. We were defeated. But there's nobility in defeat.'

Eleanor wanted to believe her father's words, but she still had to ask, 'What about Sarah?'

'I don't know,' he said, with a sigh. 'I can't imagine she would support Basker's plans to kill us. But she made her choice, and in doing so, she absolved us of the duty of saving her. I realise this may sound cold, but I'm just being pragmatic. We have to return home now, and we have to hold our heads up high.'

CHAPTER THIRTY-ONE

After some further discussion, the Kingmaker's Quartet told Jonathan and the others that they wanted to return to their castle alone. It was obvious they were feeling devastated, and the only one in the group who spent any time saying goodbye to Eleanor was James.

But even he couldn't get over their loss.

'I can't believe that they didn't let me stop and take one computer,' he said, his voice wistful. 'Just one machine. Who knows how useful it might have been.'

'You could go back,' Eleanor told him.

'Not now,' he said. 'The others just want to get home. And they're frightened of going in the tunnel again.'

'It is dark now,' said Eleanor, 'it would be more difficult.'

He nodded. 'As usual, you're the voice of reason, Eleanor. I hope things work out with your community. And I hope I see you again. Even if your group is disbanded, will you promise to come visit me?'

'Yes,' she said, 'I'd like that.'

×

After they had gone, Eleanor went upstairs to her room. She needed to spend some time alone, to think about Justin and Sarah and the pain she had felt in losing these two friends. She was surprised that she hadn't, even for a moment, considered accompanying Justin on his journey to another country. Maybe he was right, maybe he would find something out there that would make everything OK, but it seemed like cowardice to her: escaping the difficult responsibilities that lay ahead. The loss of her relationship seemed almost secondary to the disappointment she felt in Justin. For Eleanor, the only path forwards was returning to her community and convincing them of their continued importance, whatever that took. Her father was right. Justin had dragged them into something beyond their abilities. When Eleanor had ridden out on this mission, she had believed that if they weren't successful, their failure would come with enormous cost, but now that had happened, no matter how hollowed-out she felt, she believed only one thing with any certainty: that this was not the end.

Acknowledgements

Thanks to Lesley Thorne, Alexandra Heminsley,
Philippa Milnes-Smith, Suzy Jenvey and Nick Lowndes.